The e Be

Matt Beaumont is a copywriter and has been fired by some of London's leading ad agencies. He lives in North London with his wife and children.

The *e* Before Christmas

M@tt Beaumont

HarperCollins*Publishers*

HarperCollins*Publishers*
77–85 Fulham Palace Road,
Hammersmith, London W6 8JB

www.**fire**and**water**.com

A Paperback Original 2000
1 3 5 7 9 8 6 4 2

A catalogue record for this book
is available from the British Library

ISBN 0 00 711583 0 (e-book)
ISBN 0 00 711487 7 (paperback)

Set in PostScript Linotype Minion

Printed and bound in Great Britain by
Clays Ltd, St Ives plc

For the brilliant Maria

Monday
9 October
2000

Harriet Greenbaum – 9/10/00, 11.14am
to... Daniel Westbrooke
cc...
re... let's party

Dan – amidst the present flurry of activity, it seems that we are forgetting our Christmas party. This has been a remarkable year – last January nobody could have foreseen our recovery after *that* pitch. I feel we owe ourselves a bash that mirrors our achievements.

We should pull our fingers out and start planning. I believe you are ideally placed to head up a committee and get the ball rolling.

Think spectacular. The last thing I want is the usual pissed-up snog-fest in the basement car park.

Lorraine Pallister – 9/10/00, 11.44am
to... Liam O'Keefe
cc...
re... briefing

As creative sec, it is my duty to remind you that you've got the O'Malley's Microwave Fry-ups briefing in Pinki's office at 12.00. Wouldn't want my special little soldier to embarrass me and turn up late ... Lolx

Ken Perry – 9/10/00, 11.47am
to... All Departments
cc...
re... parquet flooring

You will have noted that over the weekend new laminated ash 'planking' replaced the badly worn carpet tiles in reception. To ensure that the new flooring maintains its 'as new' look for as long as possible, it is requested that all employees wearing either rubber-soled or stiletto-heeled footwear remove said shoes for the short journey from front door to lifts. It is further requested that members of account management ask their clients to comply with these instructions.

Thank you for your co-operation.

Ken Perry

Office Administrator

Liam O'Keefe – 9/10/00, 11.53am
to... Lorraine Pallister
cc...
re... briefing

As your boyfriend, it is my duty to remind you that you're on for a fuck tonight. You wouldn't want your special little soldier to be disappointed and have to bring himself off in a Kleenex, would you?

Nigel Godley – 9/10/00, 3.11pm

to... All Departments

cc...

re... Sale of the Century!

KEN HOM MIRACLE WOK

- As seen on TV
- Six-piece set, including pine spatula
- Non-stick
- Nearly new, apart from tiny scratch on Teflon
- So simple, anyone can rustle up yummy bean sprouts after a hard day at 'wok'!
- £11 ONO
- First to see will buy

Call x4667 – Nige

Harriet Greenbaum – 9/10/00, 3.36pm

to... Daniel Westbrooke

cc...

re... let's party

Dan, did you get my earlier e-mail re the party? A reply sometime *before* Christmas would be nice.

Rachel Stevenson – 9/10/00, 3.48pm

to... Nigel Godley

cc...

re... Sale of the Century!

Nigel, I thought we had agreed that, after your last Argos catalogue-style extravaganza crashed the system, we would call time on the all-staffers. You've managed to stay silent for a very creditable three months.

Let's hope that this latest e-mail is a blip rather than a reversion to old habits.

Rachel Stevenson

Head of Personnel

Daniel Westbrooke – 9/10/00, 3.54pm
to... Harriet Greenbaum
cc...
re... let's party

Profound apologies for the delay in replying but, as Director of Resource and Training, I find I am doing the work of three people. I am not complaining – far from it. The challenge of moulding tomorrow's little Greenbaums is one that I would not shirk for all the Darjeeling in West Bengal.

I agree with you wholeheartedly. This Christmas we should have a party that truly celebrates our rise from the ashes. I would love nothing more than to take on the role of MC but I fear that I am simply too snowed under to do the task justice. May I be so bold as to nominate James Gregory for the job? I believe that asking him to slip on the Miller Shanks red coat and play camp entertainments officer would give his shaky confidence a character-building boost.

Let me know if you would like me to place a fatherly arm around his shoulder and pass on the challenge.

Harriet Greenbaum – 9/10/00, 4.17pm
to... Daniel Westbrooke
cc...
re... let's party

Dan – I wasn't aware of any cracks in James's confidence. Last week, when I asked him to lead the O'Malley's pitch, he hid his insecurities well. With both that and overseeing the launch of the Real Woman Barbie range, he is far too busy to take on the party. I thought of you in that regard because, judging by the amount of lunches you have enjoyed lately, I suspected that your pre-Christmas itinerary might contain some gaps. Of course, if you are genuinely up to your neck, take me through your diary and I will relieve you of some burdens.

I am serious about wanting a party that our staff will talk about for years to come. I'm sure you won't let me down.

Daniel Westbrooke – 9/10/00, 4.30pm
to... Harriet Greenbaum
cc...
re... let's party

As long as you feel that I am the only man for the job, then, naturally, I will give the party my total commitment. Leave it with me.

Daniel Westbrooke – 9/10/00, 4.34pm
to... Susi Judge-Davis
cc...
re... extra duties

Susi, I have just been discussing the Christmas do with Harriet. I suggested we should have an event that is a little more glitzy than usual. She agrees and feels that, with my flair and experience, I am the only person she can trust to make it happen. As PA to the Director of Resource and Training, you know better than anyone how busy my duties keep me. With that in mind, I feel that, crucial though you are as my general factotum, it is time that I handed you some real responsibility.

I would like you to form a committee and lead your recruits in putting on a party that our happy family will remember for years to come. If you like, I will chair the first few meetings and, of course, I will liaise with Harriet – reporting progress, clearing the major decisions, that kind of thing.

Think big, Susi. The last thing I want is the usual embarrassing bun fight in the basement car park.

Susi Judge–Davis – 9/10/00, 4.40pm
to… Daniel Westbrooke
cc…
re… extra duties

Daniel, darling, you take on so much responsibility already that you're virtually running this place single-handedly. I'd love to take on the party and I'll get on with it straight away.

Thank you for showing such faith in me after last month's incident – you're the only one who believes me that Zoë put something in my Evian. You can count on me to organise a tasteful event that won't be ruined by the oiks in despatch acting like football hooligans – Susi

PS – I've cleared your diary tomorrow afternoon for your lunch. Who is it with?

Susi Judge-Davis – 9/10/00, 4.51pm
to… Katie Philpott
cc…
re… I'm in charge!

Hoorah!! Guess what? Daniel has put me in charge of the Christmas party!! He said that I'm the only person he can trust to make it happen. I told him it should be a really up-market do. The last thing we should have is the usual tacky affair in the basement car park. I have to form a committee but all the key decisions will be down to me. I have to decide who's on it and I want you to be my right-hand girl. Let's get together after work and brainstorm some ideas. Not at Bar Zero though – I don't want half the creative department getting in on the act – Susi

Katie Philpott – 9/10/00, 4.58pm
to... Susi Judge-Davis
cc...
re... I'm in charge!

Utterly brill! I'm fab at parties. I helped organise a charity ball in my final year at uni. Someone called Slimboy Fatty did the disco and we booked Ainsley Harriot to do the catering. It was a total pork-out and we raised over £10,000 to feed the poor little Eritrean babies. Can we do a fancy dress theme? And I know some mad games! This is going to be amazing! Why don't we go to Mash at 5.30? It's dead trendy but nice and quiet on Mondays – Katie P

liam_okeefe@millershanks-london.co.uk
9/10/00, 5.26pm
to... brett_topowlski@tbwa.co.uk
cc...
re... Yo, Beattie Boys

Do you and the boy Vin fancy beers tonight? New team started today and Pinki asked me to be nice to them. Said I'd take them for a drink, so long as I could claim it. They're called Ed and Wanda and they seem OK. Mind you, they did that daft dot com ad (the one with the glove puppets – won a bunch of awards but no fucker understood a frame of it), which means I might have to decide they're tossers. Anyway, Pinki says she'll sign for up to £50. If you're on for it we'll be in Mash at 6.30. After last Friday, can't show my face in BZ for a while.

brett_topowlski@tbwa.co.uk
9/10/00, 5.35pm
to... liam_okeefe@millershanks-london.co.uk
cc...
re... Yo, Beattie Boys

See you at Mash, if Pinki's buying. Though I wouldn't worry about showing your face at BZ – it's your sweaty Irish arse they'll remember.

Tuesday
10 October
2000

Liam O'Keefe – 10/10/00, 10.19am
to... Katie Philpott
cc...
re... last night

Just spoke to Vin and he says he's sorry about ruining your blouse. I recommend a dab of Dirt Devil for stains of unknown origin and a boil wash. Any road, what the fuck were you and the breadstick conspiring about? Haven't seen her so animated since she discovered fat busters.

Katie Philpott – 10/10/00, 10.31am
to... Liam O'Keefe
cc...
re... last night

I honestly don't know why you're so beastly about Susi. She's really sweet once you get to know her. What we were discussing is strictly confidential and had nothing to do with the Christmas party which she's in charge of organising. Whoops!!! Katie P

Liam O'Keefe – 10/10/00, 10.39am
to... Lorraine Pallister
cc...
re... you'll be delighted to learn that ...

... this year Father Christmas is a size eight (crushed velvet snow suit with silver fox trim by Nicole Farhi, ostrich skin booties by Manolo Blahnik). You got it in one, the breadstick is organising the Christmas party. That means a disco playing nothing but Lighthouse Family/M People, no alcohol and we'll get sent home at 10.30. By the way, where did you and Wanda disappear to last night? I thought I was on a promise.

Lorraine Pallister – 10/10/00, 10.44am
to... Debbie Wright; Zoë Clarke
cc...
re... piss-up in brewery

Just heard that Judge-Dredd is sorting out the Christmas party. Putting her near anything to do with fun is about as appropriate as getting Myra Hindley to baby-sit. That's the mighty Miller Shanks for you – one step forward, twenty-five back.

Susi Judge-Davis – 10/10/00, 11.16am
to... Katie Philpott
cc...
re... party plans

I can't believe we were overrun by the entire creative department last night. I hope you haven't breathed a word to any of them. Daniel swore me to utmost secrecy. Anyway, here is my suggested committee:

Susi Judge-Davis (Chairperson and Organiser-in-Chief)

Katie Philpott (Chairperson's Assistant)

Ken Perry (A total yawn but he can do all the dull admin bits)

Melinda Sheridan (Knows heaps of celebs if we want someone to do a turn)

I don't think we should ask anyone in creative. They'll only ruin it. I'll pass it on to Daniel and I think we should have our first meeting by the end of the week – Susi

Debbie Wright – 10/10/00, 11.22am
to... Lorraine Pallister
cc... Zoë Clarke
re... piss-up in brewery

Believe it or not, my mum's Auntie Glenda (you've met her, Lol – massive jugs, smells of Mr Sheen, mock-Tudor semi in Cheadle) once got Myra Hindley to baby-sit for my cousin, Billy. Says she was good as gold. Billy's a bit fucked in the head now, though, so you never know, do you? Debs

Zoë Clarke – 10/10/00, 11.25am
to... Lorraine Pallister
cc... Debbie Wright
re... piss-up in brewery

Susi organised last year's creative dept Xmas lunch. She screwed up big time!!!!! She booked us into a place called the Convent because she thought it sounded like a posh retreat. Turned out all the waitresses wore fish-nets and mini-habits!!!!!!!!!!!! And you don't want to know what a 'Virgin Mother' was!! Vince Douglas managed to do thirty of them!! Disgusting!!!!!! It was a right laugh!!! Zxxxxxxxxxx

James Gregory – 10/10/00, 11.28am
to... All Departments
cc...
re... Barbie launch

The mould-breaking range of dolls, Real Woman Barbie, goes
on sale today. This is a first for the agency, since our team was
responsible for initiating the product concept as well as the
advertising. Pinki Fallon was the driving force and deserves
huge credit. Hers and Liam's commercials break on
Nickelodeon and Cartoon Network this morning and CITV
this afternoon. They are brilliant and, since you'll all be hard
at work while they're on, we'll be showing them in reception
at lunchtime.

The Mattel guys are thrilled with our work and they have
agreed to make the dolls available to Miller Shanks employees
at trade prices. If you've got kids, take your pick:
- Bi-Barbie – a pair of dolls, Barbie and Lois, featuring 501s,
  Doc Martens and no. 2 crops.
- Burst Pipe Barbie – featuring dirty fingernails and tool
  bag, including fully adjustable tap wrench.
- Teenie Mom Barbie – set includes three mixed-race babies
  and a benefit claims game for two or more players.
- House Hubby Ken – an all-new Asian dad, complete with
  working Electrolux.

The dolls are also unique in that they are 'anatomically correct'. If you're interested, my PA, Debbie, has all the details.

Nigel Godley – 10/10/00, 11.43am
to... Rachel Stevenson
cc...
re... rank hypocrisy

I have just read James Gregory's all-staff memo regarding the sale of Barbie dolls (which, I must say, sound highly inappropriate for impressionable children, but I'll leave that for the moment). Why is it that he is allowed to sell his goods via e-mail, whereas I am not? It seems that there is one rule for high-and-mighty account directors and another for those in the 'unfashionable' accounts department.

Nige

Rachel Stevenson – 10/10/00, 11.49am
to... Nigel Godley
cc...
re... rank hypocrisy

Nigel, do I really have to explain?

Daniel Westbrooke – 10/10/00, 12.01pm
to... Susi Judge-Davis
cc...
re... party committee

I have just had a moment to review the list you left on my desk. The names seem appropriate in the main. Despite your understandable misgivings, I really think that you need representation from the creative contingent. However, I would steer well clear of the yob element that seems to hold sway on that floor.

Check my diary before you arrange your first meeting – my schedule is looking increasingly frenetic.

daniel_westbrooke@millershanks-london.co.uk
10/10/00, 12.09pm
to... si.horne@aol.com
cc...
re... lunch

Si, just to confirm our little liaison today. I have cleared my afternoon so we can have a long chin-wag. I have much to tell. Standards here really have slipped since that unwashed harridan assumed your throne. Have you seen her new Barbie films? Frightful.

I may be a little later than 1.00 – a cab to your favourite taverna in Primrose Hill can take a while. That is something else we should discuss. As your friend, I must tell you that you have nought to be ashamed of. I sincerely believe that sufficient time has elapsed for you to show your face at the Ivy once more.

Daniel

brett_topowlski@tbwa.co.uk
10/10/00, 12.24pm
to... liam_okeefe@millershanks-london.co.uk
cc...
re... Strap-on Barbie

Me and Vin were watching *Thomas the Tank Engine* on Nick (it was fucking research, all right? We had to check out Michael Angelis for a VO) and we saw one of your new Barbie ads. Nearly as horny as the stunt you pulled with Hunniford in the Freedom spot. Vin went straight to the bog to jack off. Does that Lois doll really have pierced nipples? Talking of dykes, I'd watch Wanda. Young, gifted, and blagging your bird. I'd put your foot down, unless you've negotiated picture rights.

Susi Judge-Davis – 10/10/00, 12.39pm
to... Pinki Fallon
cc...
re... party

Pinki, I am forming a committee to organise this year's Christmas do and it would be lovely to have a volunteer from the creative dept. However, it will be really boring and I am sure you are all terribly busy as per usual, so I would understand totally if you can't help out. In fact, forget I ever asked. Sorry to bother you.

Susi

liam_okeefe@millershanks-london.co.uk
10/10/00, 12.43pm
to... brett_topowlski@tbwa.co.uk
cc...
re... Strap-on Barbie

Don't worry about me. Lol promised that if she ever gets off with another bird, I can watch from the wardrobe as long as I'm quiet.

Just had a tasting session in the boardroom – Microwave Fry-ups from O'Malley's of Sheffield. 900g of saturated fats, spitting hot in under two minutes. They make Pot Noodles taste like something Marco Pierre White rustled up to impress Michelin. Now Pinki and me have got to write ads for the shit. The pink vegan can't even look at the serving suggestion without weeping for the little piggies that selflessly gave their lives in the cause of raising our cholesterol levels. I'm definitely on my own. Fucked before I start.

Pinki Fallon – 10/10/00, 2.34pm
to... Susi Judge-Davis
cc...
re... party

No bother at all, Susi. We'd love to give you some help with the party. I was going to loan you Liam, him being the leading party animal on this floor. But how about Ed and Wanda? They're our new duo and it would be a good way for them to get to know everyone. They're very big on team work, so I think they'll do a great job for you. And you get two for the price of one … ☺

Debbie Wright – 10/10/00, 3.33pm

to… Lorraine Pallister
cc…
re… Wicked Wanda

I'd slap a twenty-four hour guard on your fanny, girl. She's a certified rug-muncher. See attached – Debs

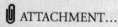 ATTACHMENT…

Wanda Bragg – 10/10/00, 3.29pm

to… Debbie Wright
cc…
re… dollies

hi
im the new copywriter
met in mash last nite
can u get me 3 bi-barbies
please
take it off salary if u can
w&a

**si.horne@aol.com
10/10/00, 5.15pm**

to… daniel_westbrooke@millershanks-london.co.uk
cc…
re… thank you, compadre

Thank you for taking me back to the age when advertising was a more genteel calling.

Thank you for your tales of Miller Shanks. They served to remind an old war-horse that he does not miss his days as your Executive Creative Director.

Thank you for standing by me. You remain one of the few who has since Celine so precipitously left the marital futon.

Thank you for your exhortations to climb afresh into the saddle and join battle once again with *les diables creatives*.

But, nay, nay and thrice nay, I shall not be tempted.

My sojourn with the Benedictines of St Gerald's taught me that I should now be concerned with less temporal matters.

These days my needs are simple, more frugal.

I am the *paysan* of Primrose Hill.

Besides, my manuscript is with my agent and I feel that it is only a matter of time before I am negotiating serialisation with the *Sunday Times*.

You and Peggy must break the unleavened with me one evening soon. I am experimenting with some dishes from the highlands of Kurdistan.

We will have to make do with lamb sweetbreads, however – goat's testes are impossible to source in NW1.

Si

Rachel Stevenson – 10/10/00, 5.26pm
to... Susi Judge-Davis
cc...
re... the Christmas party

Susi, please find attached an e-mail I received a short time ago from Nigel Godley. You would be doing me a massive favour if you got him off my back by going along with his wishes – I am finding that dealing with him takes up a good 25% of my day. Thanks! Rachel

 ATTACHMENT...

Nigel Godley – 10/10/00, 4.48pm
to... Rachel Stevenson
cc...
re... blatant discrimination

I hear on the grapevine that Ms Judge-Davis is putting together a Christmas party committee. I notice that she is packing it with her 'friends' and, as usual, *completely ignoring* us hard-working 'slaves' in accounts. I will not stand for it and I demand representation. If I am not satisfied in this matter, I will have no hesitation in taking it to the top. I am sure that James Weissmuller in New York would share my outrage.

Nige

Susi Judge-Davis – 10/10/00, 5.33pm
to... Katie Philpott
cc...
re... who's blabbed?

How come the whole world seems to know about the party committee? Someone (no doubt, that so-called 'art director', Liam O'Keefe) has already written something obscene about it in the toilets and now that stupid Godley wants to be on the committee. I certainly haven't told a soul. Well, Katie?

Katie Philpott – 10/10/00, 5.37pm
to... Susi Judge-Davis
cc...
re... who's blabbed?

How awful, Susi! Haven't said a word. You know me. You could trust me with your life. And I don't know why you dislike Liam so much. He's really a cuddly teddy once you get to know him – Katie P

Friday
20 October
2000

Katie Philpott – 20/10/00, 4.15pm
to... Daniel Westbrooke; Susi Judge-Davis; Ken Perry; Melinda
    Sheridan; Ed Young; Wanda Bragg; Nigel Godley
cc...
re... PARTY COM, 1ST MEETING, MINUTES

Time:	20/10/00, 11.00am – 1.25pm
Venue:	Boardroom
Present:	Susi Judge-Davis (chair), Katie Philpott, Ken Perry, Melinda Sheridan, Ed Young, Wanda Bragg, Nigel Godley
Absent:	Daniel Westbrooke

Susi Judge-Davis opened proceedings by thanking those attending and conveying Dan Westbrooke's apologies for being unable to re-schedule a previously booked lunch appointment. The meeting then moved on to items on the agenda.

<u>DATE:</u>

After much discussion, a date of Thursday 14 December was agreed.

VENUE:

Susi Judge-Davis felt that we should secure a five-star venue, such as the Dorchester, the Grosvenor House or the Ritz. Ed Young and Wanda Bragg felt that a more fashionable night club might better reflect the aspirations of a 'cutting-edge ideas company'. Nigel Godley said that he knew of an excellent and well-appointed church hall in Balham. Ken Perry argued that the basement car park had always been perfectly adequate and also represented more prudent use of company funds. After much discussion it was agreed that Susi Judge-Davis would investigate the price and availability of the Dorchester and Wanda Bragg would look into suitable clubs. Both will report back to the committee and a decision will be taken at a later meeting.

THEME:

A number of themes were discussed. Suggestions included Vicars and Tarts (Katie Philpott), the Nativity (Nigel Godley) and Catwalk Kings and Queens (Susi Judge-Davis). Ed Young and Wanda Bragg felt strongly that fancy dress was 'passé' and that people should be allowed to dress as they wished. After much discussion, a decision was deferred until a later meeting.

ENTS:

Melinda Sheridan said that she had contact with a number of show-business personalities. She agreed to look into their availability on 14 December. Nigel Godley said that his vicar knows Cliff Richard's manager and offered to investigate his willingness to perform. Ed Young and Wanda Bragg said that they knew a number of DJs and up-coming bands who could be available for reasonable prices. Ken Perry said that, in the past, turns by members of staff had always proved to be great fun and represented a more prudent use of company funds. It was agreed that Melinda Sheridan, Ed Young and Wanda Bragg would make inquiries and report back at the next meeting. Nigel Godley said that he would check out Cliff Richard anyway.

CATERING:

There was no time to discuss this and the meeting finished for lunch.

Ed Young – 20/10/00, 4.21pm
to... Katie Philpott; Susi Judge-Davis
cc... Wanda Bragg
re: PARTY COM, 1ST MEETING, MINUTES

Corrections:

1. Venue: what I said was, 'If Miller Shanks wanted to come on like a poncey merchant bank with a plum up its arse, it'd go to the Dorchester.'
2. Theme: I didn't feel fancy dress was 'passé'. (Words with accents are for tossers.) I said it was for 'sad cunts who had to hide their inadequacies behind a Groucho Marx moustache'.
3. Ents: you missed out my remark that if anyone put me in the same room as Cliff, I'd douse the bastard in lighter fuel and torch him like a holy Christian martyr.

Next time you report my comments, get them right – Ed

Ed Young – 20/10/00, 4.24pm
to... Liam O'Keefe
cc...
re: Susi

Amazing that a human being can be that fucking irritating. If she was on *Big Brother* her housemates wouldn't wait a week to vote her out. They'd smother the daft cow with a fucking pillow on day one.

Nigel Godley – 20/10/00, 4.25pm
to... Katie Philpott
cc...
re: PARTY COM, 1ST MEETING, MINUTES

Just a minor thing. It's *Sir* Cliff Richard. These little matters of protocol are important, don't you think? Nige

Wanda Bragg – 20/10/00, 4.26pm
to... Lorraine Pallister
cc...
re: y didnt u tell me ...

... that susi is so uptight
?
has she got stick up arse
?
+ godley
is he really that geeky
or is he ironic
+ im missing pt
?
by the way
that top makes your tits look kool
w&a

Melinda Sheridan – 20/10/00, 4.27pm
to... Susi Judge-Davis
cc...
re: a little tip

Darling, I've made a career of dealing with creative gangsters like Ed and Wanda. If I were you, I would smile regally, nod at their every whimsy and then discreetly ignore them. Take it from an old lag, it works a treat. And don't be so frightened of Wanda. I am sure you look far too straight for her tastes. Don't worry, dear heart, the chances are the next meeting will be a Caribbean cruise by comparison.

Mel

Liam O'Keefe – 20/10/00, 4.28pm
to... Lorraine Pallister
cc...
re: tonight

You on for *Ai No Corrida* at the NFT tonight? Look, when it's got subtitles it's not porn, it's Art. By the way, I could eat your tits in that top.

Zoë Clarke – 20/10/00, 4.30pm
to... Daniel Westbrooke
cc...
re... party, party!

Dan, Harriet wants to know how plans for the Christmas party are going. Can you let us know? And, if I can make a suggestion, don't skimp on the JD!!!!! Zxxxxx

Lorraine Pallister – 20/10/00, 4.36pm
to... Liam O'Keefe
cc...
re: tonight

Since when did I have a problem with porn? It's Art that fucks me off. And you're the second person with the tits thing. The first actually made it sound like a compliment ... Lolx

Daniel Westbrooke – 20/10/00, 5.23pm
to... Zoë Clarke
cc...
re... party, party!

I would have thought that your mistress would have the courtesy to ask me, as Director of Resource and Training, personally rather than charge her minion with the task. Nevertheless, you may inform her that I chaired the inaugural committee meeting today and it went exceedingly well. A number of very bright ideas were proposed and mulled over in an atmosphere of creative bonhomie. These will be further pondered and honed and, by the next meeting, we will have drawn up a definitive plan of action.

By the way, I prefer to be referred to as Daniel.

Zoë Clarke – 20/10/00, 5.25pm
to... Daniel Westbrooke
cc...
re... party, party!

By the way, I know!!!!!!!!!

rowena_hegg@hegglit.co.uk
20/10/00, 5.40pm
to... si.horne@aol.com
cc...
re... *To Byzantium, Byzantium, Where The Angels Are Decked With Rubies – A Novel*

Dear Simon,

Slightly bothersome news, I am afraid. Nick Sayers at HarperCollins has just returned your manuscript. He regrets that they cannot find room for it on their list at this time. Like

Picador and Hodder before him, he feels that the market is not quite ready for the fictive memoir of a Byzantine harp tuner. I must say that I am surprised he did not seize on it. He is usually such a perspicacious little penguin and his misjudgement saddens me.

On the plus side, he found the portrait of Petros, the transvestite concubine, particularly finely wrought. To quote him, 'it was as if the author knew him intimately'.

As I stressed when we set out on this quest, I suspected that your work would be a little elevated of brow for many a publisher. Do not be too downhearted, my sweet. As your agent, my belief in you is total. And, if it will lift your spirits at all, my sister, Letitia, endlessly bemoans the fact that your talents are lost to advertising.

I will continue to plug away.

Best,

Rowena

Harriet Greenbaum – 20/10/00, 5.49pm
to... James Gregory
cc...
re... Barbie

James – I think we need to have a talk about how Pinki's brainchild is going. I've had Mattel's CEO on the phone. He was none too thrilled with the LOONY LEFT MOVE FROM HACKNEY TO TOY GIANT piece in the *Mail* this morning. I'm around till late, so stop by.

James Gregory – 20/10/00, 6.10pm
to... Harriet Greenbaum
cc...
re... Barbie

I know all about it. I've spent the afternoon with their PR agency discussing our response. I'll see you in a few minutes.

liam_okeefe@millershanks-london.co.uk
20/10/00, 6.31pm
to... brett_topowlski@tbwa.co.uk
cc...
re... tonight

Lol blew me out for the Jap hard-core experience, so are you and Vin up for a livener at Mash? Items on tonight's agenda:

1. Ed: shaping up nicely as departmental ferret. Small, agile and extremely vicious. He's pushing Susi to the limit. Soft target, I know, but it earns him points all the same.
2. Wanda: I know she wouldn't touch me with a ten-foot Arab Strap, but I think I fancy her – she's Chaka Khan with a nice arse. And the way she and Lol are flirting – filthy minxes.
3. Horne sighting: apparently spotted with Desperate Dan in a north London Greek. Unreliable source, so could be one of those Elvis-in-a-Burger-King-in-East-Grinstead scenarios.
4. O'Malley's Microwave Fry-ups – Sheffield's big, fat prick up the arse of healthy eating. You tossers got any spare ideas for an old mate? I'm totally brain-fucked and the pitch is next Tuesday. Pinki's too vegetarian/enraged by the right-wing backlash to PC Barbie to be much use.

Later, advertising braves.

brett_topowlski@tbwa.co.uk
20/10/00, 6.36pm
to... liam_okeefe@millershanks-london.co.uk
cc...
re... tonight

See you there. As for O'Malley's, we haven't had time to piss,
let alone dream up ideas for your greasy spoon in a
microwave bollocks.

liam_okeefe@millershanks-london.co.uk
20/10/00, 6.39pm
to... brett_topowlski@tbwa.co.uk
cc...
re... Mash, 7.30

Cheers, matey, you've only cracked it.

Thursday
2 November
2000

james_f_weissmuller@millershanks-ny.co.us
2/11/00, 2.56pm (9.56am local)
to... harriet_greenbaum@millershanks-london.co.uk
cc...
re... European CEO's Conf

Harriet – my apologies for messing you around, but events here are conspiring against me. The American Advertising Association's Golf Weekend in Palm Springs falls on 5/6/7 Jan – the same time as our planned Euro get-together. It would be political suicide for me to miss the tee-off, so how would it grab you if I proposed that we shunt the conference to pre-Christmas? Say 12/13/14 Dec? I am asking you first since you are playing hostess and doubtless you will have some logistical shuffling to do. Let me know what you think before I inform your European colleagues.

By the way, I don't think I've mentioned how fitting it is that you are MC for the shindig. You have led London through a storming turnaround and nobody deserves the honour more.

And congratulations on the O'Malley's Microwave Fry-ups win. It is the icing on an already impressive cake. As a Yank, 'A GREASY SPOON IN YOUR MICROWAVE' is well beyond my understanding but well done to your team.

Hearty best wishes,

Jim

PS – One minor fly in the ointment. The Mattel people Stateside are a little jittery about the consumer boycott of your new Barbie range. What is this Association of Conservative Mothers? Some kind of terrorist front?

Harriet Greenbaum – 2/11/00, 2.59pm
to... Zoë Clarke
cc...
re... panic time

My office now. Bring my diary and a big notepad. And lend me your emery board, please. I've broken another bloody nail.

harriet_greenbaum@millershanks-london.co.uk
2/11/00, 3.19pm
to... james_f_weissmuller@millershanks-ny.co.us
cc...
re... European CEO's Conf

Jim – I'd be delighted to accommodate. 12/13/14 Dec sounds ideal. It means you are all in London for our Christmas party. We are planning something of a spectacular this year. The extra VIPs will just add to the occasion. Go right ahead and spread the word to my fellow delegates.

It was great news about O'Malley's. It moved us up to sixth in the new business table in today's *Campaign*.

Don't worry about Barbie. The boycott is a three-day wonder. The Association of Conservative Mothers is not worth worrying about – a bunch of blue-rinse worthies that no-one pays attention to. Apparently they think Hitler was soft on social issues.

I look forward to seeing you immensely. Roll on the 12th. And watch those bunkers.

Harriet

Harriet Greenbaum – 2/11/00, 3.25pm
to... James Gregory
cc...
re... Barbie

James – I've just told Weissmuller that the boycott is a storm in a teacup. Please, please, please reassure me that this is a fair assessment.

Harriet Greenbaum – 2/11/00, 3.36pm
to... Daniel Westbrooke
cc...
re... stop fucking with me

Dan – since I charged you with organising the Christmas party I have heard nothing but vague mumblings. In fact, the one concrete piece of information that I have is the date. This just happens to coincide with the re-scheduled Euro CEOs' talking shop. So, as well as the 235 employees of Miller Shanks London, you now have twenty-six Continental bigwigs plus Jim Weissmuller's entourage to whom to show a good time.

I would like a fully formed party plan on my desk by Monday morning, latest, and it had better make joyous reading.

I came into this job on a touchy-feely ticket. But fail me in this simple task and, believe me, I am quite capable of making David Crutton seem like a Care Bear.

The rocket is up your arse, Dan. I have only to light the blue touch paper.

Harriet

James Gregory – 2/11/00, 3.45pm
to... Harriet Greenbaum
cc...
re... Barbie

I wish you had talked to me first. Apart from hotspots like Brighton, Real Woman Barbie sales are abysmal. It gets worse, I'm afraid. Wirral Education Authority is being taken to court under Section 28. Apparently one of their nurseries bought a job lot of Bi-Barbies as teaching aids. A mate at C4 also told me that the *Adam and Joe Show* is using Barbie, Lois, House Hubby Ken and a My Little Pony to tape a hard-core re-make of *The Horse Whisperer*. (When you think about it, Lois does look a bit like Kristin Scott Thomas.)

Back-pedalling and putting the blame on Mattel is not an option – not after the ANDREA DWORKIN OF ADLAND piece on Pinki in Monday's *Guardian* media section.

I suggest a further crisis meeting and stiff whiskies all round. Shall I put it in your diary?

James

Daniel Westbrooke – 2/11/00, 3.47pm
to... Susi Judge-Davis
cc...
re... party

Some four weeks ago I handed you the undemanding yet important task of making arrangements for the Christmas party. To date I have heard not a dicky-bird about developments.

Now James Weissmuller tells me that the twenty-six heads of Miller Shanks's European offices, as well as the great man himself, are also to attend. If this is not sufficient incentive to pull up your socks and get to work, then I am at a loss as to what is.

I expect a fulsome progress report on my desk by tomorrow *before* I leave for lunch.

I honestly thought that you were mature enough to handle this responsibility, Susi. Do not let me down.

Ken Perry – 2/11/00, 3.52pm
to... All Departments
cc...
re... repairs to parquet flooring

Due to the excessive scuffing that has occurred to the ash 'planking' in reception, the lobby area will be closed to pedestrian traffic for the duration of tomorrow while remedial work is carried out. All staff, clients and other visitors are requested to enter and exit the building via the delivery entrance to the rear, where a temporary reception desk will be in place.

In closing, I commend you to follow the instructions issued in my note of 9/10/00 (re parquet flooring) in order to avoid a repeat of this inconvenience.

Thank you for your co-operation.

Ken Perry

Office Administrator

Susi Judge-Davis – 2/11/00, 3.55pm
to... Katie Philpott
cc...
re... aaaaaggggghhhhh!!!!

What am I going to do? Daniel just told me that all the
European CEOs *and* James Weissmuller are coming to the
Chrissy party. He said he wants a plan by tomorrow. We
haven't even had our second committee meeting yet! The
only possible venue was the Dorchester and that's probably
gone by now. This can't be happening. It's not even my fault,
is it? But everyone will blame me. They always do. I can't cope
with this. I think I'll just resign.

Katie Philpott – 2/11/00, 4.00pm
to... Susi Judge-Davis
cc...
re... aaaaaggggghhhhh!!!!

Nightmare, nightmare! But calm down, Susi. Meet me in Bar
Zero in five mins and we'll talk it through, girly to girly. Chin
up. We Philpotts never say die! Katie P

rowena_hegg@hegglit.co.uk
2/11/00, 4.04pm
to... si.horne@aol.com
cc...
re: *To Byzantium, Byzantium, Where The Angels Are Decked
      With Rubies – A Novel*

My dear Simon,

I am in receipt of further rejection slips from Little Brown
and Penguin. They, like the rest, seem incapable of spotting a
Booker certainty when it is pinching them on their *derrières*.

I do think we are in for a long old haul, Si. Perhaps, whilst we await the emergence of a more enlightened publisher, you should take up Letitia on one of her offers. She tells me that you have not responded to her latest call. She is certain that McCann Erickson's little outpost in Botswana is crying out for your leadership.

I know that you are resolute in not returning to advertising but my sister and I are only concerned for your financial well-being.

Keep well, my sweet.

Rowena

Daniel Westbrooke – 2/11/00, 4.10pm
to... Harriet Greenbaum
cc...
re... party

Harriet, you got there seconds before me. I was about to e-mail you that I am just applying the final flourish to the party plan. Come Monday morning I will make you a presentation that will fill you with the festive spirit.

I am sorry I have not been back to you sooner but I am disappointed to say that the committee let me down. As usual, I am having to do the vast bulk of the work myself. The creative representatives must bear the brunt of the blame. They have been wilfully obstructive.

I have no wish to cast aspersions in the direction of a fellow member of senior management. However, I must ask what Pinki was thinking when she recruited a copywriter who does not even possess the common decency to punctuate. How I lament the passing of the age when a writer wended his way from Oxbridge bearing only an honed wit, a shag-filled briar and a well-thumbed copy of Fowler's *Modern English Usage*.

However, I digress. I will speak to Zoë and diarise a time.

Daniel

James Gregory – 2/11/00, 4.15pm
to... Pinki Fallon; Liam O'Keefe
cc... Harriet Greenbaum
re... silver linings, lack of

As is often the way after a successful pitch, our client has had second thoughts on our creative work. He thinks the greasy spoon concept gives an insufficient nod to his company's proud Sheffield heritage. I did point out that all our focus groups showed that Sheffield rated below Scunthorpe for fine cuisine but he was adamant. I think he secretly wants a thirty-second version of *The Full Monty*.

I've put together a fresh brief. We'll have to move bloody fast if we're still going to make the air dates.

I'm sorry, guys. It was great work and I really tried to save it.

James

Wanda Bragg – 2/11/00, 4.22pm
to... Susi Judge-Davis; Katie Philpott
cc...
re... party

r u ever going 2 call meeting #2
ed and i found perfect venue
called the human cesspit
an s+m club in smithfield meat cellar
better shift if u want it
got killa band 2

called spunk monkey
as yet unsigned
kinda kenny rogers meets chem bros
ed used to swap fluids with bass player
ours for 900 quid
let us know
w&a

brett_topowlski@tbwa.co.uk
2/11/00, 4.24pm
to... liam_okeefe@millershanks-london.co.uk
cc...
re... duck for cover

A bunch of angry middle-aged women in hats has just marched past our place. They're waving placards and Barbies on gibbets. I think they're heading your way. You might have trouble getting to the tube tonight.

On the subject of people on warpaths, our guru, Beattie, is well pissed with Pinki. Even with 'hello, boys' and FCUK, he never got the media blast she's been soaking up lately. Is it true she's on *Kilroy* next week? Any road, Beattie is psycho-mad. He fired his publicist this morning. I'd tell Pinki to take sanctuary with Buddha until our Trev gets himself in the papers again.

si.horne@aol.com
2/11/00, 4.32pm
to... daniel_westbrooke@millershanks-london.co.uk
cc...
re: this evening

A quickie to confirm your visit with Peggy this evening.

I cannot wait for you to taste my six-herb carp's tongue

wrapped in fennel with a paprika coulis – one of the simple yet enduring pleasures of life in rural Uzbekistan.

And you will, no doubt, be waiting to hear news of The Novel.

To Byzantium, Byzantium, Where The Angels Are Decked With Rubies is the subject of unprecedented interest. My agent and I are playing a long game and holding out for the most suitable offer.

Until sundown,

Si

Nigel Godley – 2/11/00, 4.40pm
to... Susi Judge-Davis; Katie Philpott
cc...
re... Sir Cliff!

Fantastic news, ladies! Sir Cliff has not only agreed to perform a set of five hits (including 'Congratulations' and 'The Millennium Prayer'!) at our party but he has also offered us a gold disc *and* a pair of drainpipe trousers, as worn in *Summer Holiday*, to put up for charity auction.

You have to agree that he would really put Miller Shanks on the map! Shall I go right ahead and book him?

Nige

liam_okeefe@millershanks-london.co.uk
2/11/00, 5.01pm
to... brett_topowlski@tbwa.co.uk
cc...
re... duck for cover

The mad muthas are here and they mean business. We've just been hurling abuse at them out of the windows. As I write, our in-house militant, Wanda, is dousing them with a makeshift water cannon. She managed to give the breadstick and Phat Philpott a drenching as they fought their way back into the building.

I'm not going home in a hurry. Pinki and I are on a lock-in tonight. We've got to come up with an alternative to 'GREASY SPOON'. I was made up to take all the credit for that one but now I'm just going to have to blame you.

Ed and Wanda have the brief as well, so it's competition time.

Right, five more minutes throwing the contents of the stationery cupboard at the daft cows with hats and then work. I told Pinki that if she doesn't have a half-decent idea by ten, I'll force feed her the reconstituted pig's spleen that O'Malley's call a sausage.

pertti_vanhelden@millershanks-helsinki.co.fi
2/11/00, 5.11pm (7.11pm local)
to... harriet_greenbaum@millershanks-london.co.uk
cc...
re... season cheeringness

So, my old mucker, we are renewing auld lang sins for Christmas time! And we top dog Euro admen and ladies are to be inviting to your Yule logging party. This is news of a high order. I am making sure to fill my suitcase with my own homemaking garlic and beetroot vodka. It is making any party go with a boom-bang-a-boom!

Ho, ho, ho – **Pertti**

Ken Perry – 2/11/00, 5.16pm
to... All Departments
cc...
re... emergency equipment

I would like to draw your attention to the fact that the corridor hose reels are to be used solely in the event of a conflagration. The evacuation of water into the street via said fire-fighting equipment constitutes a breach of public order legislation.

Thank you for your co-operation.

Ken Perry

Office Administrator

david_crutton@millershanks-bucharest.co.ro
2/11/00, 5.21pm (7.21pm local)
to... harriet_greenbaum@millershanks-london.co.uk
cc...
re... So, ve meet again, Ms Bond.

That was a joke, incidentally. I just got a call from Weissmuller's assistant telling me to haul my arse to London three weeks earlier than expected. And I was so looking forward to staying in Bucharest to join the Christmas queues – they're the local equivalent of the Regent Street lights. I'm actually making a great impression over here. I've doubled billings, slashed overheads and painted the offices terracotta. The people think I'm a god.

To tell you the truth, it's so fucking prehistoric here, you could stick a chimpanzee in horn rims and the indigents would think he was an MBA. But I believe the post-Stalinist squalor is bringing out my feminine side. I haven't fired a soul in over five weeks and I'm sponsoring an orphanage – yes, honestly.

How is it going in London? Is it true that Pinki has given Barbie a working vagina? I'll see for myself soon enough. I'm looking forward to it.

I don't suppose I'll ever completely forgive you for stitching me up, Harriet. I must admit, though, to grudging admiration, if only for the fact that I never saw it coming.

David

Katie Philpott – 2/11/00, 5.33pm
to... Susi Judge-Davis
cc...
re... feeling better?

Did you manage to dry yourself off? I've just spent fifteen mins under the hand drier in the ladies'! I think one of those protesters was my godmother!!

Now, I've had a little think and here's what you should do.

- Book Dorch ballroom on 14th.
- Order second most expensive menu. Tell Dan it's the priciest and you beat them down (extra brownie points).
- Suggest making highlight of evening an awards presentation. You know, most punctual meeting reports, smiliest receptionist, that sort of whatsit.
- Book DJ. Mummy used to go out with Diddy David Hamilton. Shall I get in touch?
- And what about Cliffy? I know it's Godders' idea but I actually think he's quite good, though Phil Collins is more my cup of tea.
- I'd definitely ignore all that stuff from Ed and Wanda. Sounds weird and scary.

Deep, deep breaths, Susi. You can do it, I know you can!!
Katie P

Rachel Stevenson – 2/11/00, 5.40pm
to... Harriet Greenbaum
cc...
re... more trouble

As requested, I've looked into the disturbance outside but there isn't much more I can do. I got Ken Perry to attempt negotiation, but he seems more worried about his stationery supplies ending up in the street. The ladies refuse to budge and the police don't want to move in unless it turns violent. I'm afraid Sky News, the BBC and ITN have all rolled up, so you could have some calls to field there. I am now going to attempt to cut out the provocation they're receiving from the creative department. I'll keep you posted.

Rachel

PS – I understand that Nigel Godley has joined the protest group. Shall I have a word with him re contractual obligations?

Rachel Stevenson – 2/11/00, 5.52pm
to... Creative Department
cc... Pinki Fallon; Harriet Greenbaum
re... control yourselves

I wish to put on record that your behaviour in antagonising the protesters is counter-productive. Bombarding them with company property, water and abusive language is only making the situation worse. Liam, there is at least one journalist down there who has on tape your use of the C word in an inappropriate religious context. I insist that you all return to your desks and allow Ken Perry and myself to deal with the situation.

Rachel Stevenson

Head of Personnel

Susi Judge-Davis – 2/11/00, 5.54pm
to... Katie Philpott
cc...
re... feeling better?

Katie, darling, I don't know what I'd do without you. Thank you so, so much. I phoned the Dorchester and the room is still free, so I've faxed our booking through. I'll put the rest of the plan to Daniel tomorrow. I know him, he will *adore* it. I'll make sure you get a fair share of the credit, too.

Now I am going home to do some hand-washing. That ghastly Wanda has ruined my Valentino.

By the way, I've attached an e-mail from Melinda. Who on earth is Vinnie Jones?

 ATTACHMENT...

Melinda Sheridan – 2/11/00, 4.28pm
to... Susi Judge-Davis
cc...
re... party star

I hope that this is a dream come true, sweetheart. I am on air-kissing terms with Vinnie Jones (no relation to that erstwhile runt of the Miller Shanks litter, Vincent Douglas). It turns out, come party time, the old bruiser will be in London. I've spoken to his agent and we can have him for a song. He MC-ed the Saatchi bash a couple of years ago and my sources tell me he had them wetting their Hilfiger boxers. Shall I do the necessary?

Katie Philpott – 2/11/00, 6.01pm
to... Susi Judge-Davis
cc...
re... feeling better?

Fabbo! Vinnie Jones was in *Four Weddings* or something. He used to be a sportsman. Cricket, I think. I could ask Daddy – he's mad about *A Question of Sport*. Anyway, I'd book him! See, I told you it would all turn out lovely – Katie P

Harriet Greenbaum – 2/11/00, 8.09pm
to... Rachel Stevenson
cc...
re... sorted

The frightening women have dispersed, thanks to some exceptional negotiating by Pinki, along with a guarantee of a slot on *Newsnight*. You should go home now. Book a cab and charge it. Tell Ken to do likewise, once he has finished salvaging his stores from the pavement. Thanks for everything today.

Friday
3 November
2000

Susi Judge-Davis – 3/11/00, 8.21am
to... Daniel Westbrooke
cc...
re... the Miller Shanks Christmas Party, 2000

Daniel, I know that you are locked away in grad training all morning, so I wanted you to be able to read this as soon as you returned to your desk. My party plan is now ready. Massive apologies that it has taken so long but everyone on the committee has been no help whatsoever. As usual, I have had to do literally everything myself. Anyway, I mustn't be a moaning-minnie. Here is my proposal:

DATE: Thursday 14 December 2000
TIME: 7.30pm until 2.00am
VENUE: The Grand Ballroom of the Dorchester
DRESS: Catwalk Kings and Queens
CATERING: To be provided by the Dorchester. I have
                provisionally arranged for a five-course
                dinner at £55 per head (negotiated down
                from £65). Non-vintage Champagne and

Evian water will also be served.

MUSIC: I have scheduled Sir Cliff Richard to perform
                a short set of songs. I am still finalising a DJ
                to provide the disco. Fashionable radio
                personalities, such as Diddy David Hamilton,
                are on the shortlist of possibilities.

HIGHLIGHT: A presentation of awards for outstanding
                achievement to Miller Shanks staff.
                Presentation to be made by Vinnie Jones, the
                actor and former golfer.

I do hope you like it. It took some putting together, I can tell
you. Feel free to pick holes or make suggestions. You know
me, I'm ever so thick-skinned and I won't be hurt! Susi

Daniel Westbrooke – 3/11/00, 12.13pm
to... Susi Judge-Davis
cc...
re... the Miller Shanks Christmas Party, 2000

Susi, I must say that your proposal is not bad. I may have
some Westbrookian touches to add. I will mull and get back
to you in due course. Thank you. And have a cab standing by
from 12.45 to whisk me to Orso.

Daniel Westbrooke – 3/11/00, 12.35pm
to... Harriet Greenbaum
cc...
re... party plans

Harriet, I know that you are in conference with Mattel, unruf-
fling some feathers, but I wanted you to see this as soon as
you returned to your office. We have time in your diary,
Monday AM. However, I have been burning the midnight oil
to complete my proposal and I wanted your reaction as soon
as possible. Without further ado, the unveiling:

❧

THE MILLER SHANKS CHRISTMAS SPECTACULAR 2000

DATE
Thursday 14 December 2000

TIME
Cocktails at 7.30pm, Carriages at 2.00am

VENUE
The Grand Ballroom of the Dorchester Hotel,
Park Lane, London

DRESS
Black tie

CATERING
A five-course banquet, to be provided by the Dorchester.

(I dusted off my negotiating skills and beat them down to a very reasonable £55 per head.)

MUSIC
A performance of five decades of hit tunes from
Sir Cliff Richard.

(I didn't want anyone who would scare the visiting dignitaries! I am still finalising a disc jockey to spin the hits, as they say in the clubs. Diddy David Hamilton is high on the shortlist.)

THE EVENING'S HIGHLIGHT
A presentation of awards for performance above and
beyond, etcetera, to Miller Shanks employees.
Presentation to be made by Vinnie Jones, actor and
former champion jockey.

(I suggest that you and I go into closed session and pick the winners.)

I must say that it took some putting together. However, feel free to voice any quibbles. As you know, I am ever open to honest and constructive criticism.

Daniel

Harriet Greenbaum – 3/11/00, 3.57pm
to... Daniel Westbrooke
cc...
re... the Miller Shanks Christmas Party, 2000

I have to admit, Dan, that you have surpassed yourself. This is an excellent plan. Well done. I would like you to go ahead and make the necessary arrangements, subject to clearing the final budget with me.

The awards idea is outstanding. With no disrespect to you, I will take soundings from a cross-section of staff to pick categories and winners. Vinnie Jones is a wonderful choice of MC. Mind you, I would get your facts straight before you speak to him. At six-foot plus, he was never cut out for the flat. I hate football but even I know that he played for Wimbledon.

I do have a couple of minor issues. I'm not sure about Cliff Richard. He's not exactly speed garage, is he? He and David Hamilton (at least thirty years past sell-by) are likely to become the targets of well-aimed bread rolls from Liam O'Keefe and his mates. You can book Cliff. Just balance him with someone post-Stone Age to run the disco.

And isn't black tie just a little stiff?

But thank you again. I don't think I could have faced playing

hostess to Jim Weissmuller and co in the car park. And after
the time I'm having with Barbie, it's good to know that something is going right.

Daniel Westbrooke – 3/11/00, 4.10pm
to... Susi Judge-Davis
cc...
re... the Miller Shanks Christmas Party, 2000

I have now had a chance to digest your proposal, Susi. In the
main it is splendid. Go ahead and make commitments, subject to my approval of the budgets.

I do have one little quibble on the music front. Cliff Richard
may be a little archaic. You can go ahead and book him so
long as you get somebody a tad more up-to-date to handle
the discotheque. Even an old stick like me can tell you that
David Hamilton is antediluvian.

I did wonder about your choice of theme but, upon reflec-
tion, Catwalk Kings and Queens has the requisite swanky
ring.

Incidentally, as a lifelong aficionado of the Beautiful Game,
allow me to correct you. Mr Jones played for Wimbledon.

Susi Judge-Davis – 3/11/00, 4.14pm
to... Katie Philpott
cc...
re... party!!

Told you! Daniel loves our plan. He told me to pass on his
thanks to you personally. I don't know how I can ever repay
you ... Susi

Monday
4 December
2000

Melinda Sheridan – 4/12/00, 9.33am
to... Susi Judge-Davis
cc...
re... Vinnie Jones

We have our star for 14 December! His agent confirmed only moments ago. You can always count on your Auntie Mel and her hotline to Planet *Hello!*

Said agent would just like to know whether we will write his speech or would we prefer that he did his own? There are also two small requests: can he have a car to collect him from his country seat and a room at the Dorchester, post-party? It doesn't sound too unreasonable, does it? At least he isn't asking for twenty thousand in a carrier bag and identical twin Belarussian hookers. That was a contract breaker for one illustrious luvvie I negotiated with. He got his wishes, too. Don't ask me to name him – discreet is my middle name.

Mel

James Gregory – 4/12/00, 10.02am
to... Harriet Greenbaum
cc...
re... pear-shaped Barbie

First the bad news: this morning Toys 'Я' Us told Mattel that they are to discontinue stocking Real Woman Barbie.

Now the disastrous news: Mattel has chosen to cut its losses and pull the range out of all outlets. It goes without saying that they're canning the ads. They haven't said as much, but I suspect that they will review their relationship with us.

I'm gutted about this. Sales were showing signs of taking hold and we were starting to get some half-decent press. (Did you see the *Big Issue*?) I can't believe we've been beaten by a bunch of Anne Widdecombe wannabes and the *Daily Mail*.

I called Zoë and booked your 11.30 slot. I guess we're due a post mortem.

For some much-needed light relief, I've attached Ed's and Wanda's new O'Malley's scripts. Very funny and should guarantee our client a 33% share of students' fridges.

 ATTACHMENT...

Millershanks/TV Script

CLIENT	O'MALLEY'S	AC GROUP	GREGORY
PRODUCT	MICROWAVE FRY-UPS	CR TEAM	BRAGG/YOUNG
TITLE	GUESS WHO'S COMING TO DINNER	PRODUCER	SHERIDAN
LENGTH	40"	DRAFT	1

Open on Jarvis Cocker unpacking bulging carriers in the kitchen of a Barratt semi.

JC: Been getting some shopping in. Them Rolling
Stones are dropping in for a bite. They're getting on a
bit, so I got something nice and traditional.

With a flourish he produces a box containing O'Malley's Black
Pudding, Beans and Fried Egg Feast.

JC: I found this. One of O'Malley's Microwave Fry-ups.
Mick goes mental for pig's blood.

He carries on unloading the bags.

JC: Then later that Bjork is bringing my lawn mower
back. She's dead avant garde, so I'm trying 'er with
something new and really different.

He produces a second box of O'Malley's Black Pudding,
Beans and Fried Egg Feast and presents it to camera as if to
say 'voilà'.

JC: (after a pause) Well, she's from Iceland. She'll never've 'ad black pud before.

Cut to pack shot of O'Malley's range by a grease-spattered
microwave.

OTT VO: O'Malley's Fry-ups. Sheffield's finest in your
microwave.

Cut back to Cocker in the kitchen. It's late evening and he's
scraping splattered black pudding off the wall.

JC: That were a disaster. No-one told me Bjork were a
veggie.

Millershanks/TV Script

CLIENT	O'MALLEY'S	AC GROUP	GREGORY
PRODUCT	MICROWAVE FRY-UPS	CR TEAM	BRAGG/YOUNG
TITLE	THE BROTHERS	PRODUCER	SHERIDAN
LENGTH	40"	DRAFT	1

Open on Jarvis Cocker sipping a cup of tea in a small café.
He lifts his shades and speaks earnestly into camera.

> JC: The amazing world of guitar pop – sexy, glamorous,
> sometimes strange. 'Ere's a true story …

Ripple dissolve to a bedroom in a council flat. Manchester
City posters adorn the wall. Noel Gallagher sits on the
bed with an acoustic guitar. He strums chords and struggles
with phrases, rejecting each one with increasing signs of frustration.

> NG: (singing) You gotta take it like a bloke, on the chin,
> yeah … nah … accept the rough with the smooth …
> rubbish … just go with the flow, baby … ahh, boll …

He's disturbed by the door opening. In slouches brother Liam
with a plate of O'Malley's Sausage, Egg and Chips. He hands
it to Noel with a grunt.

> LG: 'Ere's your tea, our Noel.

Liam turns and exits. Noel looks down at the plate, then calls
after his departed brother.

> NG: 'Ey, our kid, I wanna roll with it.

He stops as if struck by lightning. He hurriedly picks up the
guitar and strums excitedly.

> NG: (singing) You gotta roll with it, you gotta roll with
> it…

Ripple dissolve back to Cocker.

> JC: And you thought they nicked all their best ideas off
> the Beatles.

He looks knowingly into camera before replacing his shades
and returning to his tea.

Cut to pack shot of O'Malley's range by a grease-spattered
microwave.

> OTT VO: O'Malley's Fry-ups. Sheffield's finest in your
> microwave.

Susi Judge-Davis – 4/12/00, 10.05am
to... Daniel Westbrooke
cc...
re... Vinnie Jones

Fantastic news. Melinda confirmed that we have him for the
14th. We need to write his speech. Can I do it, please? I'd love
to give it a bash. When I worked for Si in creative, I used to
read the rubbish some of those so-called copywriters turned
out and I always thought I could do much better – Susi

Melinda Sheridan – 4/12/00, 10.10am
to... Ed Young; Wanda Bragg
cc... James Gregory
re... O'Malley's

Very droll scripts, you two. Well done. I have sent them to the
Cocker's management and we will await an answer. Should
the stroppy Mancs decline, may I put in a personal request
that you write an ad for Damon Albarn? I'm no Blur fan but
those puppy dog eyes bring out the hussy in me.

Mel

Daniel Westbrooke – 4/12/00, 10.17am
to... Susi Judge-Davis
cc...
re... Vinnie Jones

Splendid news, Susi. It is gratifying to see that all the items on
our plan are falling squarely into place. As for the speech, I
think that it would be better left with me. Without wishing to
puff on my own cornet, I still cherish my public speaking
prize from Charterhouse days. I shall blow the cobwebs from
my *Oxford Dictionary of Quotations* and throw myself into the
oratorical plunge pool.

Ed Young – 4/12/00, 10.34am
to... Susi Judge-Davis; Katie Philpott
cc...
re... what the fuck are you tarts playing at?

You never call, you never write. Wanda and I have busted guts to sort you out a band and a venue, and we've got DJs queuing up for the gig. We're still waiting for a second meeting of your poxy committee. This party is supposed to be in ten days. If you expect any more help from us you're having a laugh. Now, leave us alone, we've got work to do.

Susi Judge-Davis – 4/12/00, 10.37am
to... Katie Philpott
cc...
re... foul-mouthed pigs

I presume you read that horrid e-mail from Ed. You were so, so right when you said to ignore him and his disgusting lezzy friend – Susi

liam_okeefe@millershanks-london.co.uk
4/12/00, 10.53am
to... brett_topowlski@tbwa.co.uk
cc...
re... take it to the Bridge

Got tickets for Chelsea/Liverpool tonight (James Gregory was going to take the Mattel people but they're suddenly staying in to wash their hair).

Fancy it? Ed's coming – he was born in Hull, so, naturally, he's true-blue Chelsea. I know Vin is Everton but tell him that Heskey losing ball while tripping over rogue blade of grass guarantees him at least seventeen laughs over ninety minutes.*

Investment tip: buy, buy, buy full sets of Real Woman Barbie. Guaranteed collector status within two months.

Wanda and Ed beat us to it on O'Malley's. First rule of advertising: when in doubt, hire celebs. No, I'm being a churlish little gobshite – their scripts are half-decent. All right, they're fucking brilliant. Now stop going on about it, will you?

*Stats provided by Carling Opta.

Susi Judge-Davis – 4/12/00, 12.09pm
to... Daniel Westbrooke
cc...
re... your carriage awaits

Your taxi for Le Caprice is here. I've booked another at 2.30 to bring you back. Have a lovely, lovely time – Susi

charalambous.theocritos@dorchester.com
4/12/00, 12.25pm
to... susi_judgedavis@millershanks-london.co.uk
cc...
re... MILLER SHANKS PARTY

Dear Ms Judge-Davis,

I have tried to reach you by phone without success. I was expecting you at 11.00 this morning, as appointed, to help us co-ordinate the arrangements for your company's party this evening. The florists have arrived with the table arrangements and our production team have commenced erecting the stage. We will need you to approve the stage dressing as well as the decorations in the rest of the ballroom. Our kitchens have already begun preparations for the banquet and I will require your approval of the final selection of wines.

If there has been some unforeseen problem that has prevented your coming here, please let me know and I will do whatever I can to assist.

I am at your service,

Charalambous Theocritos

Banqueting Manager

susi_judgedavis@millershanks-london.co.uk
4/12/00, 12.36pm
to... charalambous.theocritos@dorchester.com
cc...
re... MILLER SHANKS PARTY

Dear Mr Theocritos,

You are mistaken. My booking is for *14* December, not for today. I suggest that you go back and consult your records. I will see you in ten days' time.

Yours sincerely,

Susi Judge-Davis

Executive Personal Assistant to the Director of Resource and Training

charalambous.theocritos@dorchester.com
4/12/00, 12.45pm
to... susi_judgedavis@millershanks-london.co.uk
cc...
re... MILLER SHANKS PARTY

Dear Ms Judge-Davis,

I regret to say that there has been no mistake. I have looked again at your fax and it quite clearly says 4 December 2000. I suggest that you consult your original of the confirmation letter.

Please contact me as soon as possible so that we may discuss.

Yours sincerely,

Charalambous Theocritos

Banqueting Manager

susi_judgedavis@millershanks-london.co.uk
4/12/00, 12.53pm
to... charalambous.theocritos@dorchester.com
cc...
re... MILLER SHANKS PARTY

Dear Mr Theocritos,

I did not keep the original of the confirmation. In dealing with an establishment of the calibre of the Dorchester, I did not think it necessary. This is an absolute outrage. I distinctly made the booking for the 14th. That is still the date when we intend to hold our party and I expect you to confirm that arrangement by return.

Yours sincerely,

Susi Judge-Davis

Executive Personal Assistant to the Director of Resource and Training

charalambous.theocritos@dorchester.com
4/12/00, 1.26pm
to... susi_judgedavis@millershanks-london.co.uk
cc...
re... MILLER SHANKS PARTY

Dear Ms Judge-Davis,

I would like nothing more than to be able to help. However, as early as last June Esso booked our facilities for 14 December, so there is no possibility that I or any of my colleagues would ever have offered to accommodate you on that date.

With regard to your original fax, is it not possible that you mistakenly omitted to insert the number one in front of the number four? I sincerely believe that this is probably what occurred.

It is my duty to inform you that we will expect settlement in full of your account with us.

I am genuinely sorry for your predicament and regret that there is no more that I can do to help.

Yours sincerely,

Charalambous Theocritos

Banqueting Manager

Susi Judge-Davis – 4/12/00, 1.31pm
to... Katie Philpott
cc...
re... PANIC, PANIC, PANIC!!!!

WHERE ARE YOU?

Susi Judge-Davis – 4/12/00, 1.44pm
to... Daniel Westbrooke
cc...
re... slight problem

The Dorchester is in an unbelievable muddle with the date for our party. They are telling me that 14 December is not available. I am going there now to have it out with them. In case you get back before I do, that is where I am. I am sure that once I raise my voice a little and show them I mean business, they will sort everything out. I don't think it's anything to worry about but I just wanted you to be kept abreast – Susi

david_crutton@millershanks-bucharest.co.ro
4/12/00, 2.29pm (4.29pm local)
to... harriet_greenbaum@millershanks-london.co.uk
cc...
re... Barbie

I've just seen the report of the demise of Real Pubes Barbie on Sky News. (The first thing I did upon arrival here was to have a dish installed – even the Romanians have heard of satellites, though they think they are manned by pixies.) I must say, you look very fetching on TV. The camera takes years off you.

No, I really mustn't gloat.

Anything an old colleague can do to help? David

Daniel Westbrooke – 4/12/00, 2.51pm
to... Susi Judge-Davis
cc...
re... slight problem

Well, that is quite some e-mail to read on a full stomach. I have to say that I am more than a little concerned, Susi. See me the second you return. In the meantime, you will *not* tell a soul about this sorry state of affairs.

Susi Judge-Davis – 4/12/00, 3.06pm
to... Katie Philpott
cc...
re... why aren't you at your desk?

We're in an awful mess. It isn't my fault, it really isn't, but everyone will blame me as usual. I am going to see Daniel now to explain. I wish you were here.

pertti_vanhelden@millershanks-helsinki.co.fi
4/12/00, 3.15pm (5.15pm local)
to... harriet_greenbaum@millershanks-london.co.uk
cc...
re... Barbie Dolls

I am seeing you on Sky News station trying to make a silky purse from a dog's dinner and I am feeling for your troubledness. If I may be offering some advice, we have an old saying here in Finland. It is approximately translating as 'the herring that is swimming ahead of the flock is not ending up in the pickling barrel'. This is always giving me comforts when my own radical and state-of-the-art thinkings are receiving the pooh-pooh treatment by all and sundae.

By the way, my exciting is building up for your party. I am having a two and eight deciding which reindeer antler hat to be packing.

Chirpy-chirpy-cheep-cheep – Pertti

Susi Judge-Davis – 4/12/00, 3.22pm
to... Daniel Westbrooke
cc...
re... I have never been so abused in all my life.

I must say that nobody has ever, ever spoken to me the way that you did just now. I really did not expect to be called those things by the Director of Resource and Training. I have done everything I possibly can to try to sort out this problem, which is not of my making. I am leaving now to consider my position.

Susi

pierluigi.nesta@dorchester.com
4/12/00, 3.26pm
to... susi_judgedavis@millershanks-london.co.uk
cc...
re... incident in lobby

Whilst I remain sorry for your situation, I must reiterate that I stand by Mr Theocritos in insisting that the Dorchester will not be held accountable for the mistake that has occurred. Your misguided attempt to tear up our copy of your fax clearly indicated where the blame lies in this matter.

I must also inform you that the cost of one Louis XIV mirror plus that of a new suit for Mr Theocritos will be added to the Miller Shanks account.

Yours sincerely,

P. Nesta

General Manager

Melinda Sheridan – 4/12/00, 3.28pm
to... Susi Judge-Davis
cc...
re... nag, nag

Susi, sweetheart, Vinnie Jones's punctilious agent is pressing for confirmation on the speech/limo/room matters. Any answers yet?

Katie Philpott – 4/12/00, 3.46pm
to... Melinda Sheridan
cc...
re... Susi

Have you seen her? I had an upsetting e-mail from her and
now she's disappeared. I'm worried. Katie P

Melinda Sheridan – 4/12/00, 3.59pm
to... Katie Philpott
cc...
re... Susi

I tried to reach her myself, darling. I have no idea where the
little waif is. I wouldn't over-exercise your worry muscles,
though. This is Susi we are talking about. Much as I keep a
corner of my heart warm for her, you will find her name in
the *OED* under prima donna.

liam_okeefe@millershanks-london.co.uk
4/12/00, 4.00pm
to... brett_topowlski@tbwa.co.uk
cc...
re... blue is the colour ...

See you at six in World's End for pre-match vat.

The word is that the breadstick has bunked. Done a department sweep on what tabs she's pretended to have taken this
time. My quid's on Aquaban – amusing but a long shot.

Daniel Westbrooke – 4/12/00, 4.13pm
to... Susi Judge-Davis
cc...
re... this has gone on quite long enough

I think that you have made your point now. I am sorry if I was uncharacteristically snappy earlier but this is a truly monumental fix that you have landed me in. The moment that you return, see me. We need to put heads together and conjure up a solution that will leave us both with egg-free visages.

brett_topowlski@tbwa.co.uk
4/12/00, 4.22pm
to... liam_okeefe@millershanks-london.co.uk
cc...
re... ... football is the game

World's End at six. Vin's asking for it – he's wearing his replica Gazza shirt with matching beer gut.

Breadstick update: Vin just returned from Soho porn run. On his way back he saw Susi in Patisserie Valerie stuffing her gob with chocolate gateau, with a side order of strawberry cheese-cake – things must be serious this time. When he pressed his face to the window and ran his tongue stud over the glass by way of comfort, she fled in hysterics.

Closely followed by waiter – hadn't paid her bill. It's not her day, is it?

rowena_hegg@hegglit.co.uk
4/12/00, 4.25pm
to... si.horne@aol.com
cc...
re: *To Byzantium, Byzantium, Where The Angels Are Decked With Rubies – A Novel*

My dear Simon,

Even your offer to 'proletarianise' the title to *Sing Unto Me*,

Oh Golden Harps Of The Bosphorus is not washing, I am afraid. London's publishers are going through one of their philistine cycles. We will just have to grin and bear it while they dumb down the presses with loutish fiction produced for semi-literate twenty-somethings. Such is the tragedy of being a literary agent who cut her teeth in an age when a writer knew when and when not to employ the gerund.

I hope that this experience has not embittered you, my sweet.

Best, as ever,

Rowena

david_crutton@millershanks-bucharest.co.ro
4/12/00, 4.39pm (6.39pm local)
to... james_f_weissmuller@millershanks-ny.co.us
cc...
re... Barbie

James, in the spirit of inter-office co-operation I have offered Harriet Greenbaum assistance in damage-limitation on the Barbie front. I am the first to admit that the Coca-Cola business taught me valuable lessons in that regard.

The unhappy situation with Mattel does, perhaps, highlight the need for Miller Shanks to have in place a European Chief Executive Officer. With no disrespect to yourself, I suggest that overseeing the operations of all of Miller Shanks offices around the globe, as well as the massively successful operation in the States, spreads your gifts too thinly. Delegating some of the burden to a Euro CEO would allow you to take a backward pace and keep an eye on the big picture.

The candidate for such a post would have experience in more than one European market – say, in a developed economy such as the UK, as well as in one of the emerging markets east of Berlin. If you wish, I would be happy to flesh out my ideas in more detail.

And, before you ask, no, I am not proposing myself for the job! I am having far too much fun grappling with the challenges here. Also, if I left now, I would genuinely fear for the future of my little orphans.

My very best wishes to your wonderful wife and children and I look forward to seeing you in ten days.

Kind regards,

David

Letitia Hegg / letitia@tavistockhegg.aol.com
4/12/00, 4.44pm
to... si.horne@aol.com
cc...
re: the Horne of Africa!

Darling, darling Si, is there no way on earth I can persuade you to meet with McCann's Botswana people? They have fallen head-over-heels in love with your CV. The job would be so, so you. Imagine the challenge of fashioning diamonds from bare African rock. Doesn't it just set you off into a creative drool? And their CEO, you would just adore him. Such an anglophile. He can recite Betjeman backwards and has his suits made at an exquisite tailor's in Windsor.

Just tell your favourite little head-hunter you'll give it a few moments' thought.

Letty

james_f_weissmuller@millershanks-ny.co.us
4/12/00, 5.05pm (12.05pm local)
to... david_crutton@millershanks-bucharest.co.ro
cc...
re... Barbie

David, I am glad to hear that you are tendering international aid to Harriet. Judging by my recent conversation with her, there is little more that can be done, though I should think she will be delighted to have your moral support.

On the bigger issue of European oversight, your suggestion may be the answer to our prayers. I would love to have your proposed job description in writing, in advance of the European CEO's Conference. We can discuss further when we meet in London.

I also look forward to giving thanks in person for the great strides that you have made in Romania. You are providing an object lesson in bringing capitalism to the commies.

Best wishes,

Jim

harriet_greenbaum@millershanks-london.co.uk
4/12/00, 5.12pm
to... david_crutton@millershanks-bucharest.co.ro
cc...
re... Barbie

There is little you can do from the land of Vlad the Impaler but thank you for the offer. I am sure it was well meant. At least something positive has come out of this mess. It has put the crooked smile back on that face of yours.

I'll see you in a few days. We are putting on the party at the Dorchester especially to remind you what civilisation is.

Harriet

Harriet Greenbaum – 4/12/00, 5.17pm
to... Pinki Fallon
cc...
re... don't be ridiculous

No, I will not accept your resignation over Barbie. It may have been your idea but I endorsed it. If anyone takes the shit, it will be me. Besides, I still happen to think it is a wonderful concept.

Anyway, we may be in the process of losing a client but we are surely shifting people's perceptions of what this place is capable of.

So, all in all, a good day's work. I'll see you tomorrow.

Harriet

si.horne@aol.com
4/12/00, 5.21pm
to... daniel_westbrooke@millershanks-london.co.uk
cc...
re: eternal gratitude

Thank Peggy for the gladioli she sent after our *soirée*.

I am so sorry that the yak's milk cheese brought her out in such an unpleasant rash.

And my profuse apologies for the delay in replying but I have been away with my muse. You know me when inspiration's gnat bites.

The auction for *Byzantium* proceeds apace. The figure is

reaching quite dizzying levels. It is causing me to pause and wonder whether this is really what I want.

Do I truly wish to be published?

Maybe it is simply enough to write.

My agent would be mortified were she to know of my agonising but, above all else, the artist must be true to himself.

Perhaps a return to advertising would suit me after all but, this time, more in the role of a creative missionary.

I feel the restless spirit of Albert Schweitzer calling me to Africa – somewhere like Botswana.

I shall look into it.

My fondest wishes to you both,

Si

Wanda Bragg – 4/12/00, 5.27pm
to... Lorraine Pallister
cc...
re... sorta love letter

so
u r a footie widow tonite
the ed-case + i had result on omalleys
lets celebrate
how about i cook u something w/lard
?
u northerners like that sort of shite dont u
?
+ u can kiss my pussy
cost me £160
shes blue pt siamese
w&a

Lorraine Pallister – 4/12/00, 5.34pm
to... Wanda Bragg
cc...
re... sorta love letter

Ready when you are. But be a love and make it beef dripping
... Lolx

Tuesday
5 December
2000

Harriet Greenbaum – 5/12/00, 11.22am
to... All Departments
cc... james_f_weissmuller@millershanks-ny.co.us
re... Mattel

This morning Mattel asked us to repitch for the Barbie account. We have declined to do so. Despite the adverse reaction from some sectors of society, I think that we should all feel extremely proud of the ground-breaking work we did for this client. Judging by the number of calls I am receiving from curious marketing directors who have seen the media coverage, far more good than bad will emerge.

Well done to everybody on the Barbie team.

Harriet

Zoë Clarke – 5/12/00, 11.30am
to... Daniel Westbrooke
cc...
re... party

Dan, Harriet wants an update on progress. Are you free at 12.30? Don't worry, she's in a really lovely mood!! Zxxxx

Melinda Sheridan – 5/12/00, 11.31am
to... James Gregory
cc... Wanda Bragg; Ed Young
re... O'Malley's

Good news, James. You can go into your O'Malley's presentation reasonably assured that Jarvis Cocker will come out and play. His management responded very sharpish with a positive in principle – a sure sign that their client loves the work. Now, if I can get those surly Gallaghers to appear together on celluloid, then you can rightly accuse me of genius.

Zoë Clarke – 5/12/00, 11.34am
to... Lorraine Pallister; Debbie Wright
cc...
re... Judge-Dredd

Still no sign of her. I heard she was seen eating five whole chocolate cakes!!! She's never been this bad!!!!!! Do you think she might have done it this time?!!!! And what's going on with you and Wanda, Lol? Is that lipstick on your collar?!!!!!!!!!!! Zxxxxxxxxxxx

brett_topowlski@tbwa.co.uk
5/12/00, 11.44am
to... liam_okeefe@millershanks-london.co.uk
cc...
re... wasn't that fun?

You get home all right? Vin and me were four hours in casualty before they tweezered the pebble-dash out of his forehead. Ed's got a fuck-off swing on him for a short-arse. Best keep those two apart in future.

Anyway, what are our chances of crashing your party? Vin never got to knob Zoë. He was inches away at last year's do and he fancies trying again for old times' sake. No accounting for the warped little scally's taste, is there? But, given his preference for farming matters on the Net, I guess even Zoë represents a step-up in class.

Zoë Clarke – 5/12/00, 11.56am
to... Daniel Westbrooke
cc...
re... party

Are you coming to see Harriet at 12.30 or what?

Daniel Westbrooke – 5/12/00, 12.06pm
to... Zoë Clarke
cc...
re... party

My apologies to your mistress but I will not be able to make it on this occasion. I am up to my neck with the new training programme and have yet to apply the finishing touches to 'Dos and Don'ts: Graduate Trainee Protocol, 2001'. Then there is the completion of the internal resource audit to oversee. Please tell her to rest assured that the party arrangements are proceeding to the letter of the plan. I will make bringing her up to date my very next priority.

Daniel

liam_okeefe@millershanks-london.co.uk
5/12/00, 12.13pm
to... brett_topowlski@tbwa.co.uk
cc...
re... wasn't that fun?

Got home fine. I left the feisty little twat, Ed, doing a Dennis Wise on the cabby. He's a scary fucker. He might be too short for most rides in Euro Disney but we could make a mint out of him on the unlicensed boxing circuit. How about it, Terry Lawless?

The breadstick has yet to surface. Desperate Dan's top lip is looking unusually sweaty. The rumour (started by me fifteen minutes ago) is that he's got her up the duff.

I think Lol's been a bad girl. She's acting weird today and smells of bacon and Polo Sport.

I'll get you into the party. Tell Vin he'll see his old mate, Crutton, there, so he might want to do a Puffy Combs and get tooled up.

Nigel Godley – 5/12/00, 12.17pm
to... Susi Judge-Davis; Katie Philpott
cc...
re... Sir Cliff

I am very sorry to say that Sir Cliff has pulled out from his exclusive performance at our Christmas party. The reason his manager gave to Father Clive, my vicar, is that he has no wish to be associated with a company that would promote anything as un-Christian as Real Woman Barbie.

Personally, I don't feel able to talk him round since I am in agreement with him. In fact, I will stick my neck out and state categorically that I believe the Devil himself has been at work in these offices. I only stay on to make a stand against him and all his works.

Obviously this leaves us in a pickle, *vis à vis* entertainment at our celebration of the birth of the little baby Jesus. If there is anything else I can do to help, I am ever available in my base-ment cubby.

Nige

Katie Philpott – 5/12/00, 12.24pm
to... Melinda Sheridan
cc...
re... poor Susi

She just called me on her mobile. She's round the corner in Pret à Manger. She's in a terrible state and says Dan is trying to kill her. She wants me to go and see her. Will you come, too? Pretty-please – Katie P

Melinda Sheridan – 5/12/00, 12.27pm
to... Katie Philpott
cc...
re... poor Susi

Once again I seem to be Miller Shanks' answer to Virginia Ironside. I will see you in reception in a couple of minutes.

james_f_weissmuller@millershanks-ny.co.us
5/12/00, 1.21pm (8.21am local)
to... david_crutton@millershanks-bucharest.co.ro
cc...
re... European CEO

David, your proposal was outstanding. Thank you. The Worldwide Board has discussed the matter and I am happy to say that we have reached a conclusion that is well within the ballpark of your thinking. I feel it is only fair that you be the first to know our decision. I will pull you aside when we all meet in London and let you know.

And thank you for the photos of yourself with your orphans –
tremendously moving. They will definitely be front page on
the next issue of the Miller Shanks Global Bulletin.

Best wishes,

Jim

david_crutton@millershanks-bucharest.co.ro
5/12/00, 1.34pm (3.34pm local)
to... harriet_greenbaum@millershanks-london.co.uk
cc...
re... preparations

Have Krug on ice for my arrival. I believe I will have good
news to share.

Melinda Sheridan – 5/12/00, 2.15pm
to... Daniel Westbrooke
cc...
re... Susi

Dan, I have just spent the last ninety minutes calming your
PA. Between sobs she managed to tell me everything. I am
bringing her to see you now. Before we arrive, I suggest that
you have a tumbler of that cherished XO you keep hidden on
your nick-nack shelf and take some deep, soothing breaths. I
don't want you to shout at her. I am sure that she has been a
silly-billy but blaming her will not get us a party on the 14th.

liam_okeefe@millershanks-london.co.uk
5/12/00, 2.23pm
to... brett_topowlski@tbwa.co.uk
cc...
re... la breadstick

She's been sighted rising from the dead in reception. The

unconfirmed story is that she's fucked up rotten on the party. Christ knows why anyone ever gave her an event to organise. She can't even file her nails in the right order.

Anyway, it's now Happy Meals for 235/entertainment by Ronald McDonald. You and Vin still fancy it?

Daniel Westbrooke – 5/12/00, 3.02pm
to... Katie Philpott; Melinda Sheridan; Ed Young; Wanda
    Bragg; Ken Perry; Nigel Godley
cc...
re... meeting

I have decided to call an emergency session of the Christmas Party Committee. It will take place in the boardroom at 4.00 sharp. Unfortunately, my duties as Director of Resource and Training mean that I am indisposed. Susi is under the weather, so, in both of our absences, Melinda has kindly agreed to take the chair. Please give her your full support.

Daniel

Melinda Sheridan – 5/12/00, 5.51pm
to... Katie Philpott; Ken Perry; Nigel Godley; Ed Young;
    Wanda Bragg
cc... Daniel Westbrooke
re... party

Thank you, darlings. That was a more successful little summit than I could have hoped for. I am sure that the same whiff of can-do pluck was prevalent at Dunkirk. Now to business. Here is the battle plan:

VENUE:
I have made a whirlwind check. As we suspected, all suitable arenas have been snapped up. Wanda, I really don't think that –

your S&M club will suit our purposes. Believe it or not, I have been. While I had a charming time, I would not want to take the Worldwide President of Miller Shanks Inc. Besides, the environmental health people would have fun there – I don't believe they wash the blood from their manacles.

So, once again, the basement car park it is. Ken, you have been there countless times before. You know what to do. Just remember to clear away the recycling skip this year – the despatch boy who fell asleep in it last time wasn't found for thirty-six hours. His mother was worried unnecessarily.

DÉCOR:

Katie, you are a treasure. Drafting in your auntie is an excellent idea. She does sterling work on ITV's *Dream Rooms*. Her interiors have a cobbled-together quality that is perfectly suited to a one-off event. Make the call to her. And don't sneer, Ed. If you would prefer to have Philippe Starck hang the baubles, then feel free to try him.

FOOD:

Katie, call your very good friend, Ainsley, and ask him to pack his garlic press. If he is not available, then it is plan B and as many cases of O'Malley's Microwave Fry-ups as we can lay hands on.

DRINK:

Don't worry, Ed, there will be gallons of it.

BAND:

In the absence of pop's Peter Pan, we have a gap to fill. I almost felt a consensus emerge for Ed's friends, Spunk Monkey. Under the circumstances, 'almost' will do. Book them, Ed. Just do one thing for me: vet their CVs for membership of any satanic cults. It will help Nigel sleep a little easier.

DISCO:
Wanda, call Terry Coldwell and ask him to whirl the wheels of steel. I take your word that he earns big respect in the UK garage scene, whatever that is. Incidentally, was he the one in East 17 who appeared not to do a great deal but oozed buckets of pheromones in not doing so?

ETCETERA:
The awards presentation will take place as planned. I will notify Vinnie Jones of the downgrading of venue. I know him and he will put up with slumming it a little – he used to play for Wimbledon, after all.

As for the theme, we will stick with Catwalk Kings and Queens. It would be nice for Susi to feel that she has still made a small yet significant contribution.

That's all for now, troops. You know your tasks and I will speak with each of you daily for progress reports. And let's be nice to each other. (That includes you, Ed.)

Mel

Melinda Sheridan – 5/12/00, 5.56pm
to... Katie Philpott
cc...
re... nursemaid duty

An extra chore for you, Katie. You know how fragile Susi is, so please keep an eye on her. And get her involved with the party a little. Have her choose the colour of the balloons or something – nothing too responsible.

Melinda Sheridan – 5/12/00, 5.59pm
to... Daniel Westbrooke
cc...
re... next step

As you will have read, the party is now in safe hands. You know me – reliant is my middle name. I am now going to see Harriet to break the news to her as gently as possible. Stick around and I'll let you know how it goes.

Wanda Bragg – 5/12/00, 6.03pm
to... Melinda Sheridan
cc...
re... kool meeting

«lets do the party right here»
u were born 2 lead
luv u like a train
w&a

Nigel Godley – 5/12/00, 6.32pm
to... Melinda Sheridan
cc...
re... a matter of principle

For the last hour I have been wrestling with my conscience and I have decided that there is only one course of action open to me.

I am sorry to let you down at this time of crisis but I must resign from the committee. I cannot condone the hiring of a popular music group whose name I cannot even bring myself to type.

I will return, a sadder man, to the unglamorous but essential task of reconciling invoices.

Nige

Melinda Sheridan – 5/12/00, 6.41pm
to... Daniel Westbrooke
cc...
re... brace yourself

That bumper copy of the *New Yorker* on your coffee table – I would stuff it down the seat of your pants, pronto. Harriet wishes to see you.

Thursday
14 December
2000

Melinda Sheridan – 14/12/00, 11.16am
to... Daniel Westbrooke
cc...
re... get a bloody move on

Vinnie Jones's agent has called six times this morning to ask where his client's speech is. Daniel, this is the one little thing that you are doing for the bash tonight. And before you utter a word, don't tell me how busy you've been. I caught sight of your diary yesterday. It contains enough open white space to make Ranulph Feinnes salivate and strap on his crampons.

Melinda Sheridan – 14/12/00, 11.19am
to... Katie Philpott
cc...
re... chop, chop

Katie, when is your blessed aunt going to show up with her bloody staple gun? Ken Perry has been hanging around in the car park for over an hour. Even he has better things to do. Call her and tell her to hurry up. And, if it will stop you cluttering up my voicemail, then, yes, Susi can send a special party all-staffer. If that's all it takes for her to feel that she has master-minded this bloody event, then she's dafter than any of us thought.

Melinda Sheridan – 14/12/00, 11.26am
to... Ed Young; Wanda Bragg
cc...
re... music

I have finally listened to the Spunk Monkey demo. While I applaud anyone who can rhyme 'Catholicism' with 'jism', I think we should ask them nicely to curb their wilder lyrical excesses. And, Wanda, I am sure that Terry Coldwell has spent a lifetime in Brooklyn-by-Walthamstow perfecting his gangsta snarl but would you mind asking him to stay sweet when he receives the inevitable requests for 'Three Times a Lady'?

Melinda Sheridan – 14/12/00, 11.29am
to... Nigel Godley
cc...
re... no

Nigel, we cannot find room in a corner of the car park for your Nativity scene. I don't care how many matchsticks you used to build it.

Katie Philpott – 14/12/00, 11.32am
to... Melinda Sheridan
cc...
re... chop, chop

Auntie Viv has just arrived. She's terribly sorry but her RAV 4 was overloaded with MDF and she was pulled up by the

police in Victoria. I'll calm her down with a nice cup of tea
and take her to Ken. And I'll tell Susi the good news. She'll be
so chuffed – Katie P

Harriet Greenbaum – 14/12/00, 11.37am
to... Zoë Clarke
cc...
re... jobs

1. Pick up my party dress from the cleaners.
2. Find a meeting room for JFW for 2.00 today. He wants a
   chat with DC. And this time make sure that JFW's
   travelling humidor is present, correct and ***switched on***.
3. Call the Marriott and have them shift either one of our
   men from Athens and Istanbul to another floor. Putting
   them in adjacent rooms was not a smart move.
4. Call BA and obtain an assurance that our Italian CEO's
   right to a seat in their VIP lounge will not be questioned
   on his return flight. Copies of papers proving his lineage
   to Lucrezia Borgia are on your desk.
5. Find out if JFW's new Purdey is ready for collection. He
   has helpless creatures to kill the moment he returns
   Stateside.
6. Get me some Librium. Someone in the office must have a
   bottle – this is an advertising agency.

I'll see you after my speech. Please God that, for once, you sta-
pled the pages in the right order.

Harriet Greenbaum – 14/12/00, 11.48am
to... Melinda Sheridan
cc...
re... please tell me it'll be OK

JFW has been taking masterclasses in pomposity and DC is
being insufferably smug. The comedy Finn and his new chum

from our Düsseldorf office are larking about like Rik and Ade in *Bottom*. This lot are impossible. In fifteen minutes I have to stand before them and speak about the implications of the single currency on pan-European ad budgets. God help me. This bloody conference is doing my head in. Melinda, please tell me that you have the party so buttoned down that tonight I'll be able to take refuge inside a bottle of scotch and fuck the lot of them.

Zoë Clarke – 14/12/00, 11.50am
to... Lorraine Pallister
cc...
re... what the hell's a Purdey?

I thought it was a hairdo. Why would Weissmuller want one?

Melinda Sheridan – 14/12/00, 11.53am
to... Harriet Greenbaum
cc...
re... please tell me it'll be OK

At this very moment everything is a total pig's ear. It still will be at 7.00. But don't worry, it'll be right as rain by 7.29. Good luck with your presentation – give 'em hell, ecu-warrior! Mel

Susi Judge-Davis – 14/12/00, 12.04pm
to... All Departments
cc...
re... THE EVENT OF THE MILLENNIUM!

DEAR SUPERMODELS. TONITE, AN EVENING OF FINE DINING, DANCING AND ENTERTAINMENT FROM THE STARS OF SHOWBUSINESS!!!

LIVE MUSIC BY CHART TOPPERS,

Pink Monkey

DANCE THE NITE AWAY TO THE SENSATIONAL SOUNDS OF
Tony Coldwell
(FORMERLY OF TEEN HEART THROBS, BOYZONE)

SPECIAL GUEST SPEAKER...
STAR OF STAGE, SCREEN AND WIMBLEDON'S CENTRE COURT,
Vinnie Jones

VENUE ... THE FASHION FANTASY GROTTO (BASEMENT CAR PARK)
CREATED BY TV'S VIVIAN PHILPOTT
STARTS AT 7.30
YOU'D BE TOTALLY, TOTALLY BONKERS TO MISS IT!!!

Melinda Sheridan – 14/12/00, 12.11pm
to... Rachel Stevenson
cc...
re... favour

Is there any way in the world that you can have IT put a temporary block on Susi's e-mail before she heaps me with any more pink-tinged embarrassment? I'll owe you – Mel

Daniel Westbrooke – 14/12/00, 12.13pm
to... Susi Judge-Davis
cc...
re... speech, speech!

Susi, find attached my final draft of Mr Jones's speech. Melinda has been pestering for it but she does not seem to appreciate that these things cannot be hurried. Run off copies and distribute to her and to Harriet for her approval. Mind you, I very much doubt that she will find even a comma that she wishes to change.

📎 ATTACHMENT...

A speech for Mr Vinnie Jones – final draft

My lords, ladies and gentlemen, it gives me more than a frisson of pleasure to be in your midst on this bejewelled eve.

Back in the days when I humbly plied my trade on the greensward, little did I imagine that there would come a time when I would be standing before advertising's highest achievers – a group for whom the motto of Her Majesty's Airforce, *per ardua ad astra*, might have been coined afresh.

If I may continue the aeronautical allusion for a moment, allow me to take wing alongside you, as you soar o'er snow-kissed peak and swoop 'neath towering bank of cumulus, for I wish to revel in your Icarian accomplishments.

Tonight is an occasion to award those amongst your brethren who have set new altitude records in making the vertiginous ascent to advertising perfection.

I will now hand over to your great leader: your Boudicca; your Maid d'Orléans; the one who elicits the cry, 'for Harry and for England'.

Or rather, 'for Harriet' ...

[pause for laughter]

... Harriet Greenbaum will now summon forth the deserving winners.

All that remains for me to say is that a few hours hence, when dawn's chorus calls time on the bacchanalia, slip homewards to sleep.

'To sleep, perchance to dream.'

For it is the dreamers that have builded here this shimmering edifice of creative possibility.

[applause]

Melinda Sheridan – 14/12/00, 12.16pm
to... James Gregory; Ed Young; Wanda Bragg
cc...
re... O'Malley's script meeting

Jarvis's agent has confirmed our 4.00. Lord only knows why I scheduled this meeting for today of all days but we are stuck with it.

Good news on the brothers grim. Liam and Noel remain adamant about not appearing on set together. However, Liam has agreed to be shot on a separate day and we can drop him in in post-production. The punters will never see the joins and our clients won't notice the extras on the invoice, the amount they are already spending on this.

One tiny gnat in the ointment. Much as he adores the scripts, Jarvis has a rabid hatred of 'Roll With It' – too Status Quo, apparently. He says you can have any Oasis song apart from that. What think you, Ed and Wanda?

Liam O'Keefe – 14/12/00, 12.18pm
to... Susi Judge-Davis
cc...
re... wow!

Top e, Susi. Vinnie Jones, the elegant master of serve and volley! Fantastic! Do you think he'll reminisce about the time he duelled on Centre Court with Neil 'Razor' Ruddock in that epic five-setter? Can't wait.

Susi Judge-Davis – 14/12/00, 12.23pm
to... Katie Philpott
cc...
re... Liam

You were so, so right about him. He really is a sweetie! And he
loves tennis, just like me! Susi

Melinda Sheridan – 14/12/00, 12.25pm
to... Harriet Greenbaum
cc...
re... don't do this to me

If you haven't done so already, read the copy of the speech
that Susi left with you. Then, if you think of me as a friend at
all, tell me you've filed it in the bin. If I have to hand that
piece of twaddle over to Vinnie Jones, then I honestly fear for
my life.

daniel_westbrooke@millershanks-london.co.uk
14/12/00, 12.31pm
to... si.horne@aol.com
cc...
re... lunch

I have spent the morning with my nose in Jancis Robinson
and I have discovered the perfect wine to toast the new
Executive Creative Director of McCann Erickson Botswana. It
is uncorked and rooming at the Ivy as I type. I will see you
there at 1.30.

It is so like you to turn your back on the publishers' feeding
frenzy and heed the call of the savannah. I cannot wait for
you to expound.

Talking of matters literary, I shall bring along my own little
dabbling. It is short and sweet but I would treasure the opinion of a true smith of words.

Daniel

Ed Young – 14/12/00, 12.33pm
to... Melinda Sheridan
cc... Wanda Bragg; James Gregory
re... O'Malley's script meeting

I loved Pulp. Not any more. Cocker can fuck off. I don't give a
shit-caked blanket how many records he's sold, tell him to
stick to writing songs. We do the ads. He's not the only pop
star from Sheffield, you know. We'll have that Phil Oakey
from Human League or the bastard with big hair from Def
Leppard.

Melinda Sheridan – 14/12/00, 12.40pm
to... Ed Young
cc...
re... O'Malley's script meeting

As ever, you're the dulcet voice of reason, Ed. Why don't you
tell him yourself at 4.00? I'm sure he'll take it well – in his line
of work he'll be used to disagreements over musical differ-
ences.

Katie Philpott – 14/12/00, 12.41pm
to... Susi Judge-Davies
cc...
re... Liam

Told you he was a snuffly Pooh Bear! Are you ready to go?
God, I'm sooooo excited!!!!!! I know we're not getting Nicky
Clarke himself but I've heard all his stylists are the absolute
dog's doodahs! I've spent the last hour fussing around Auntie
Viv and my hair is a total fright! Still, by 2.30 I'll be a cuddly
Kate Moss!!

Susi Judge-Davies – 14/12/00, 12.42pm
to... Katie Philpott
cc...
re... Liam

I've just finished drawing a design – you know hairdressers, they can't understand a thing unless it's in pictures. So thicko.

The new, calm, bridge-building me is in super-drive. I'll just get rid of Daniel, then I've got one more e to send. I'll meet you in reception in five mins – Susi

Susi Judge-Davies – 14/12/00, 12.44pm
to... Harriet Greenbaum
cc...
re... Daniel Westbrooke

Just a small thing, Harriet. As a special secret surprise, do you think you could single Daniel out with an award tonight? I wanted to nominate him as the sweetest, most hard-working, cleverest person this agency has ever, ever been lucky enough to have. I know he'd hate the attention but he so, so deserves it. If you don't want to be accused of favouritism, I wouldn't mind presenting it myself.

Lorraine Pallister – 14/12/00, 12.57pm
to... Wanda Bragg
cc...
re... 10, 9, 8 ...

All the girls are doing pre-party bollocks this lunchtime. How many fucking frocks can they try on? Fancy BZ and we'll get mildly lubed while they're tit-arsing around?

Nigel Godley – 14/12/00, 1.03pm
to... All Departments
cc...
re... first things first

I realise that the whole agency is excited about the party but I should remind you that time sheets for the month ending 30/11/00 must be in by 10.00 tomorrow. Failure to do so will result in the withholding of personal expenses. Parties have their place but, as you are all aware, work must come first.

Nige

Wanda Bragg – 14/12/00, 1.07pm
to... Lorraine Pallister
cc...
re... 10, 9, 8 ...

no can do
ed + i r twiddling w/omalleys pre jarvis
cant stop for beer
+ anyway
u + me alone in bz
people will talk
+ we wdnt want that
now wd we
?
w&a

Ken Perry – 14/12/00, 1.35pm
to... All Departments
cc...
re... A SAFE PARTY IS A HAPPY PARTY

In order to enable tonight's event to proceed without incident, please note the following.

Since the car park is normally a no-smoking zone, the detectors are especially sensitive. I would therefore ask you to ensure that, throughout the course of the evening, there are never more than two smokers per 50m^2.

I am sure that if we all respect this, the overall levels of enjoyment will be enhanced rather than diminished.

Thank you for your co-operation.

Ken Perry

Office Administrator

James Gregory – 14/12/00, 1.57pm
to… Harriet Greenbaum
cc…
re… this is interesting

Check out *Time Out*. A gay club in Brixton is having a BYOB night tomorrow. Nothing funny about that, you might think, only the last B stands for Barbie. Due to the scarcity of the product, they're challenging everyone to find an RWB and bring her along, otherwise no admission. Any PR in this?

Harriet Greenbaum – 14/12/00, 2.04pm
to… James Gregory
cc…
re… this is interesting

Sounds good but I'm too knackered to think about it, to be honest. I've got five minutes break before the buffet lunch for twenty-six Euro-bosses. Call Caitlin Jones at the *Standard* (we went to school together) and give her my regards. She'll probably be interested in the BYOB snippet. She'll keep it MS-friendly, if she doesn't want her husband to know what I do about her 18th birthday party.

Harriet Greenbaum – 14/12/00, 2.07pm
to... Melinda Sheridan
cc...
re... don't do this to me

Don't fret. Said speech was flushed down the executive pan a couple of minutes ago. I'll put together some bullet points for VJ – he can improvise on those. How will I find the time, you ask? I need something to keep me awake when JFW delivers his keynote address this afternoon.

By the way, you can also hand VJ the task of making the awards. I have lock-jaw from public speaking today. Tonight I'm going to join the despatch boys, get royally rat-arsed and have them teach me those Posh Spice football songs.

Harriet Greenbaum – 14/12/00, 2.11pm
to... Susi Judge-Davis
cc...
re... Daniel Westbrooke

You've got more front than I credited you with, Susi. How can I put this tactfully? You and Dan are lucky that I am not docking the Dorchester's astronomical bill from your salaries. Your boss will not receive an award tonight.

And, while I'm at it, you can inform him that his speech ranks with IKEA assembly instructions in the pantheon of bad writing. He should stick to what he knows, whatever that is.

Harriet Greenbaum – 14/12/00, 2.13pm
to... Zoë Clarke
cc...
re... if you ever get back from trying on party dresses ...

... or whatever it is you're doing, pick up the sealed envelopes that are in my top drawer and deliver them to Melinda. And no sneaking them via the kettle in the kitchen.

Ken Perry – 14/12/00, 2.24pm
to... Melinda Sheridan
cc...
re... slight confusion

Am I to understand that you have authorised Vivian Philpott to drape fabric from the car park ceilings, thereby obscuring the sprinkler nozzles? I have pointed out to her that this is in clear breach of fire regulations. I would be grateful if you could clear this matter up.

Ken Perry

Office Administrator

Lorraine Pallister – 14/12/00, 2.39pm
to... Wanda Bragg; Liam O'Keefe
cc...
re... see me

I've just bumped into Zoë with a stack of gold envelopes. Had a blinding party idea. Better than the pig's blood in *Carrie*. Stop whatever you're doing. Need your creativity. Say nowt to no one.

Wanda Bragg – 14/12/00, 2.42pm
to... Lorraine Pallister
cc...
re... see me

got a pause b4 our meet with jc
on my way
talking of carrie

can i b john travolta
+ receive oral favours
in rtn 4 help?
w&a

Melinda Sheridan – 14/12/00, 2.43pm
to... Katie Philpott
cc...
re... emergency

One of your fellow trainees tells me that you are having a
shampoo and set. You should be here helping to get this show
on the road. The moment you return, head for the car park
and take your rampant kinswoman in hand. She has already
threatened Ken Perry with a cordless drill.

Ed Young – 14/12/00, 2.55pm
to... Melinda Sheridan
cc...
re... spunk's up

Band's here. They're unloading their gear in reception. Ken's
getting irate about his planks. Told him to piss off, this is rock
'n' roll. Anyway, they want to do a soundcheck. Can I send an
all-staffer asking everyone to keep the noise down?

And, before you ask, Cocker is still a towering twat. We're not
changing a fucking thing.

liam_okeefe@millershanks-london.co.uk
14/12/00, 3.14pm
to... brett_topowlski@tbwa.co.uk
cc...
re... sightings

1. A very smug Crutton leaving private meeting with Tarzan F Weissmuller. Just how smug? Sources reckon he looked like he'd got Tarzan not only to suck him off but to swallow as well. Seems his exit visa from Romania has come through.
2. Tear-streaked breadstick walking back into building wearing tea-cosy hat. Presumed hair calamity.
3. Closely followed by Phat Philpott looking ... wait for it ... fucking adorable. Kate Moss's double (i.e. if Kate Moss went on a Big Mac and Pop Tart diet).
4. Ed in the bogs trying on various pairs of pop star shades for the imminent arrival of Mr Pulp himself.
5. Mad woman off pony TV makeover show chasing Perry through reception with routing chisel.

Any road, work to do now. Lol's commissioned me and Wanda to help out on a party stunt. Stay conscious for it – it's a gold, love.

James Gregory – 14/12/00, 3.27pm
to... All Departments
cc...
re... Jarvis Cocker

In a short while the lead singer of Pulp will be here for a meeting on O'Malley's Microwave Fry-ups. Signing him up for this campaign is a fantastic coup both for us and O'Malley's. Much of the credit must go to Wanda and Ed, whose scripts he loves, and to Melinda, who's so persuasive she could probably get Linford Christie to endorse the BNP.

While we should all rightly be excited about this, I do have one small request. Please don't clog up reception with your autograph books. When Aqua came in for Coke last January, it was like Wembley Arena down there. Let's all be thrilled, but cool!

Thanks,

James

Debbie Wright – 14/12/00, 3.50pm
to... Lorraine Pallister
cc...
re... rover's return

Just back from the shops. Can't wait to show you my dress – it's so see-through I'll need a full fanny wax! I got Zoë a present. A pair of those wobbly jelly bra implants from la Senza. If Vin's crashing the party with Brett tonight she needs all the help she can get! Saw Susi in the bogs. What happened to her hair? Looks like she's had a blow-dry with a welding torch – Debs

Debbie Wright – 14/12/00, 3.56pm
to... Zoë Clarke
cc...
re... boob job

Come and get your new tits!

Melinda Sheridan – 14/12/00, 4.01pm
to... James Gregory; Ed Young; Wanda Bragg
cc...
re... he's here

Run along to Meeting Room 1 now. I hope you've all scrubbed up nicely. And, Ed, a soapy mouthwash wouldn't go amiss.

Zoë Clarke – 14/12/00, 4.09pm
to... Debbie Wright
cc...
re... present

Can't come and see you now. Harriet doesn't want her office unguarded for a sec. She thinks all these foreign CEOs are kleptos or something!!!!!!!!!!!!!!!!!!!!!!!!!! It's a real pisser – I wanted to sneak down to reception and get a look at that singer from Radiohead!!!!! Zxxxxxxxxxxx

Rachel Stevenson – 14/12/00, 4.16pm
to... All Departments
cc...
re... working hours

I know that you are all dying to squeeze into dresses etc but I have to remind you that we don't officially stop work until 5.30. I'm sorry to be a Scrooge but we do have VIPs here from all over Europe/USA and we don't want to look unprofessional.

Rachel Stevenson

Head of Personnel

PS – Don't all laugh, but I'm going as Jean Shrimpton tonight. If anyone else is planning the same, it was my idea first!

brett_topowlski@tbwa.co.uk
14/12/00, 4.47pm
to... liam_okeefe@millershanks-london.co.uk
cc...
re... sightings

Me and Vin are almost ready to rock. Everyone's favourite scally is slapping on CK1 (suitcase on Oxford St variety) and he's toting a johnny with Zoë's name on it (literally – I saw him write it on in Magic Marker). He scored some top toot at lunch time – you'll have Daniella Westbrook's* nose by midnight but it'll be worth it for the buzz. Are you sure you can sneak us in? I know Miller Shanks isn't the Bank of England but look at your track record. You said you'd get us backstage at the Britney gig and that bouncer nearly had Vin's knackers for earrings.

*She couldn't possibly be related, could she? No, far too silly.

Harriet Greenbaum – 14/12/00, 5.12pm
to... Melinda Sheridan
cc...
re... last minute changes

As we were leaving our session, JFW asked me if he could take the stage for ten minutes this evening to make a 'Major League' announcement. I suggest we slot him in before Vinnie Jones and hope that whatever he has to say doesn't upstage our own presentations. I have a horrible feeling that it has something to do with DC – his self-satisfaction level has risen to a new high this afternoon.

I'm sending Zoë down to you now with the bullets for VJ. Incidentally, did the envelopes arrive safely?

Melinda Sheridan – 14/12/00, 5.26pm
to... Harriet Greenbaum
cc...
re... last minute changes

The envelopes landed in my in-tray while I was hobnobbing with Jarvis Cocker (went better than expected – I'll fill you in later). Tell Mr Weissmuller I will slip him into my running order.

You will be pleased to hear that, despite frequent tantrums and a slight graze inflicted to Ken Perry's bald patch, Katie's aunt actually has the car park looking rather festive in a low-ceilinged, subterranean kind of way. All right, it isn't the ball-room at the Dorchester but after a few crème de menthe frappés it won't look like an NCP either.

si.horne@aol.com
14/12/00, 5.34pm
to... daniel_westbrooke@millershanks-london.co.uk
cc...
re... the fondest of farewells

Thank you for a splendid time, Daniel.

One that tasted all the more savoury for knowing that Ms Greenbaum would be signing for it.

It was the perfect way to bid adieu to the first world.

My flight takes to the air on Sunday and I shall be sharing my Yuletide meal with the elephants.

I leave you with some *bons mots* of encouragement.

Your little speech caused tears to well. You really must write. A talent such as your own should not be allowed to wither on the vine of graduate training.

You and Peggy *must* visit me soon in the bush. I have already made some research into *la cuisine locale*. They do remarkable things with termites.

Your friend,

Si

Zoë Clarke – 14/12/00, 5.59pm
to... Debbie Wright; Lorraine Pallister
cc...
re... help!!!!!!!!!!!!!

Has anyone seen my other implant thingy?!!!!! I look bloody stupid with just one!!!!!!!!!!!!!!!!!!!!!!!!!!!!!!!!!!!! Zxxxxx

Lorraine Pallister – 14/12/00, 6.02pm
to... Zoë Clarke
cc...
re... help!!!!!!!!!!!!!

I think I just saw one of the despatch boys playing keepy-uppy with it in the corridor.

James Gregory – 14/12/00, 6.12pm
to... Harriet Greenbaum
cc...
re... O'Malley's – top line

Terrific meeting. I was worried about Ed's attitude but he was sweetness itself. He even suggested a small change to the Oasis script. It now features O'Malley's Offal Platter ('Liver Forever' – geddit?). By the way, I talked to your friend and I think we'll get a small feature on Barbie in the *Standard* next week.

daniel_westbrooke@millershanks-london.co.uk
14/12/00, 6.20pm
to... si.horne@aol.com
cc...
re... the fondest of farewells

I am so glad that you enjoyed our luncheon. It was heartening to see you facing down those who snickered behind napkins at your entrance. British advertising will be the poorer without your courageous presence.

Thank you for your erudite appraisal of my work. Sadly, yours is not an opinion shared by the lowbrows at Miller Shanks.

Still, I will struggle on.

Bon voyage.

Daniel

Wanda Bragg – 14/12/00, 6.25pm
to... Lorraine Pallister
cc...
re... u ready yet

im in costume
going as naomi campbell crossed w/divine brown
«i dont get **into** bed for less than 10 grand»
wot about u
?
crap meet w/jc
ed sold out w/corniest idea since the sunshine breakfast
thats ed 4 u
v talented
but a ☆-fucker
w&a

Katie Philpott – 14/12/00, 6.33pm
to... Susi Judge-Davis
cc...
re... it really isn't that bad

Please, please, please don't go home, Susi. No one will laugh, honestly. I'm sure I could salvage it with a bit of gel, and those little clip whatnots from Accessorize. Call me. The party just won't be the same without you!!!! And I bet you any money they'll give you an award – Katie P

Pinki Fallon – 14/12/00, 6.36pm
to... Creative Department
cc...
re... my shout

If you're all in your glad rags, meet me in Bar Zero for a pre-party drink. We're a beautiful bunch of people and we deserve it ... ☺

Harriet Greenbaum – 14/12/00, 6.54pm
to... All Departments
cc...
re... HAPPY CHRISTMAS

I just want to say have a fantastic party. Eat, drink and be bloody merry. I know I will be.

Nigel Godley – 14/12/00, 11.59pm
to... All Departments
cc...
re... time sheets

I know the majority of you will be 'tripping the light fantastic' but, should you return to your desks to collect coats, bags, etc, why not spare a moment to complete those outstanding time sheets? It may seem a chore but you'll thank me in the morning when the hurly-burly of work takes over again.

Nige

Friday
15 December
2000

james_f_weissmuller@millershanks-ny.co.us
15/12/00, 6.17am
to... harriet_greenbaum@millershanks-london.co.uk
cc...
re...

Harriet,

I have just done two extra circuits of the Marriott gym in an attempt to work the stench of last night out of my system. I am sorry to be so blunt but I am deeply disappointed. You know well enough that I am no puritan, far from it. I am all in favour of high-jinks but where is your sense of proportion?

I thought that you, of all people, would host an evening that would not bring our great business into such disrepute. My only hope now is that our new European Chief Exec will be able to keep a lid on such shaming excesses.

Now I have to deal with David Crutton who is beating down my bedroom door. What is it with you Brits?

We will speak before I leave this morning.

James

James Gregory – 15/12/00, 8.56am
to... Melinda Sheridan
cc...
re... lost and found

Just got here and found a barely conscious body under my desk. He's got a big, bushy moustache and he's mumbling what sounds like Polish – I'm assuming he's our Warsaw CEO. I don't want to bother Harriet with it – enough on her plate. Shall I put him in a cab to Heathrow?

PS: what do you think of our new Euro Führer? It'll bring back memories, if nothing else.

Harriet Greenbaum – 15/12/00, 9.02am
to... Zoë Clarke
cc...
re... last night

I appreciate that this is probably a little early in the hangover for you to make an appearance. Shortly I am leaving for the Marriott to bid farewell to our foreign friends. When I return at about 11.00 I would like to spend some moments alone with you. You know what I would like to discuss.

You can also arrange for Melinda and Dan to see me. And tell Ken Perry I need a full damage report.

Harriet Greenbaum – 15/12/00, 9.07am
to... Rachel Stevenson
cc...
re... personnel issue

I arrived this morning to find the attached e on my machine. It confirms what I have long suspected. Susi would use up all three lifelines on the opening question of *Who Wants To Be A Millionaire?* and still get the answer wrong. Is there any way we can have her transferred to licking stamps?

 ATTACHMENT…

Susi Judge-Davis – 14/12/00, 10.12pm
to… Harriet Greenbaum
cc…
re… thakyou!!

i was so overcom with emotion i had toflee to my desk to recover! i thouht id write you a not wile i was here. it was so so sweet of youto giv danniel a award. i shoud ave nown yor email erlier ws only fooling. i am so gullllible!!!! i couldnt uderstand aword what vinie jons was sayin inhis presetation (i rember him as realy wel-spoke wen he won wibledon!) but iam sure it was verrry touchhing! i havent hada chanc tospeak to danel yet but I bet hes as thrilld as i am. thank yu harit!

ps sory aboutthe speling but i is a bit squiffy!!

Harriet Greenbaum – 15/12/00, 9.13am
to… Melinda Sheridan
cc…
re… last night

At some point Zoë will schedule a meeting. Between now and then you might like to come up with explanations for the following:
1. The awards. Giving Dan the Simon Horne 'Let's Do Lunch' Memorial Plate, while apt, was not my idea. What the hell happened to those envelopes?
2. The band. What on earth possessed you to book a bunch

of degenerates who'd have been rejected by Baader-
Meinhof as too anarchic? Spunk Monkey! Didn't the
bloody name give you a clue?
3. Vinnie Jones. Will he sue over the thick lip? One day I will
   laugh at the bizarre notion of Westbrooke landing that
   punch. Just not today.

I am sorry if I am sounding like your boss rather than your
friend but JFW has already been on my case and patience is in
short supply.

Melinda Sheridan – 15/12/00, 9.48am
to... James Gregory
cc...
re... lost and found

You're right, keep your Lech Walesa lookalike well out of
Harriet's line of sight. I noticed yesterday that she had Big
Jimmy Weissmuller's new shotgun propped by her filing cabi-
net. The mood she is in, she won't hesitate to use it. I am due
on with her later to face the music. 'Happy Days Are Here
Again'? I think not.

Zoë Clarke – 15/12/00, 10.10am
to... Lorraine Pallister
cc...
re... what am I going to do??????????????!!!!!!!!!!!!!!!!!!!!!!!!

Harriet wants to see me at 11.00 about you know what!!!!!!!!!!!
What am I going to say?!!!! You've really landed me in it!! And
I feel awful!!!!! Sick three times on the Bakerloo line!!!!!!!!!!!!!

Katie Philpott – 15/12/00, 10.13am
to... Susi Judge-Davis
cc...
re... you party monster!!!

I know I told you to 'let your hair down' last night but you went wild!!! I've never seen anyone dance like that!!! Not surprised you're not here yet!!! Call me as soon as you arrive. If I'm not at my desk, I'll be in the car park. I have to sort out Auntie Viv. She's hopping mad with Ken Perry. He took down her lovely ruched hangings at 4am. She's brought a photographer in this morning to snap them for her new book (*Vavoom Your Room With Viv*!!). Anyway, find me – Katie P

Lorraine Pallister – 15/12/00, 10.15am
to... Zoë Clarke
cc...
re... what am I going to do?????????????!!!!!!!!!!!!!!!!!!!!!

Calm down. It's a piece of piss. Say you took the envelopes straight to Mel's and left them in her in-tray. End of story. Don't worry, you're a brilliant liar. I heard you faking it in the ground floor ladies'. It didn't fool me – our Vin was way too pissed to make anyone come ... Lolx

PS: What do you think of the new Euro Boss? Rumour is he'll be based in London. He'll need a sec and I know he loves you!

Lorraine Pallister – 15/12/00, 10.18am
to... Wanda Bragg
cc...
re... where were you?

Thought I was supposed to be crashing at yours last night. I lost Liam as well, so no plan B. I last saw him dancing with that new PA in TV (you know the one – 'I really want to work in *film*, darling'), so he'd better have a fucking good story. Apart from that, top party, eh? Told you Miller Shanks was *Hi-de-hi*, minus canned laughter … Lolx

Wanda Bragg – 15/12/00, 10.24am
to… Lorraine Pallister
cc…
re… where were you?

sorry
needed 2 b alone
missed my brookie x tho
wdnt worry about liam
last time i saw him w/tv tart he was glazing over as she said «im just waiting for sammy 2 start his next feature + im outa here»
sam mendes
or fireman sam
?
bollox either way
see u at lunch 2 compare parties
w&a
ps
whos this new euro ceo
?
he looks scary

Zoë Clarke – 15/12/00, 10.31am
to… Lorraine Pallister
cc…
re… what am I going to do?????????????!!!!!!!!!!!!!!!!!!!!!!!

THAT WAS NOT ME WITH VINCE DOUGLAS!!!!!!!!! I swear on my life!!!! His aftershave gave me a rash after one snog and I couldn't go near him!! Zxxxxxxxxxxxxxxxxxxxxxxx xxxxxxxxxxxx

Lorraine Pallister – 15/12/00, 10.45am
to... Debbie Wright
cc...
re... whodunit?

All right, was it you with Vin in the ladies'? If not, who? Zoë swears blind it wasn't her and I believe her. Well, she was gagging for it, so why would she lie? Lolx

Nigel Godley – 15/12/00, 10.58am
to... All Departments
cc...
re... time sheets

Since so many of you (188, to be precise) have still failed to hand in your time sheets, I am about to do a floor walk and collect all the outstanding ones. Please have them signed and ready.

And, while I am online, can whoever left talcum powder scattered all over my desk last night please refrain from using my work station as a beauty parlour? It is hard enough as it is to maintain a tidy ship.

Nige

Liam O'Keefe – 15/12/00, 11.00am
to... Lorraine Pallister
cc...
re... g'morning

You get home OK last night? Before you ask, I didn't get up to anything. I crashed at Brett's.

Debbie Wright – 15/12/00, 11.02am
to... Lorraine Pallister
cc...
re... whodunit?

Haven't a frigging clue. I saw Rachel Stevenson looking flushed in a post-shag kinda way but she wouldn't, would she? Has anyone asked Vin?

Lorraine Pallister – 15/12/00, 11.04am
to... Liam O'Keefe
cc...
re... g'morning

Spoken like a bloke with a clear conscience. I'm beginning to wonder about you and Brett. Anyway, see you later. Pinki wants me to spend an hour on the Net looking for non-Christian Christmas carols. (Look, I just do as I'm told, OK?) In the meantime, ask Vin who he was poking last night. It wasn't Zoë.

liam_okeefe@millershanks-london.co.uk
15/12/00, 11.09am
to... brett_topowlski@tbwa.co.uk
cc...
re... alibi

If anyone (i.e. Lol) asks, I crashed at yours. You can stop tutting. I was so gobsmacked that this one came through, I couldn't possibly say no. And I feel terrible about it. Honest. I probably won't be able to sleep or whatever happens to people who feel terrible. Talking of pulling, ask Vin who he was slipping it to. There's a lot of interest back here. Gotta go now. There's some Secret Squirrel-type stuff to do. Full SP on last night later.

Zoë Clarke – 15/12/00, 11.17am
to... Lorraine Pallister
cc...
re... phew!!!!

Just seen Harriet. Not sure she believed me but I stuck to my story and there's not much she can do!!!!!!!!! My hangover's wearing off and it's all coming back to me!! A scream!!!!!!!! I've never seen Susi pissed!!! Did you see her chuck that potato at the Crettin?! She was almost human!!!!!! And that scrap!!!!!!! I know Desperate Dan can't take a joke but I never thought he'd swing for Vinnie Jones!!!!!!!!!!!!!!!! Zxxxxxxx

Harriet Greenbaum – 15/12/00, 11.20am
to... Zoë Clarke
cc...
re... consider yourself warned

I meant what I said a few moments ago. If I find out that you had anything to do with last night's fiasco, you'll be out so fast, you won't have time to pack up your nail polish. Now have Melinda come up.

Nigel Godley – 15/12/00, 11.21am
to... All Departments
cc...
re... those prizes in full

Yo Homies,

Since Ms Greenbaum so uncharitably spoiled last night's festivities by breaking up the special awards presentation when it had barely got under way, I thought it only fair that you should know the winners in full.

- DANIEL WESTBROOKE – THE SIMON HORNE 'LET'S DO LUNCH' MEMORIAL PLATE
- PINKI FALLON – THE BUZZ LIGHTYEAR PLATINUM MOON BOOT FOR SERVICES TO TOYS
- VINCE DOUGLAS – THE JONATHAN AITKEN AWARD FOR COMPLETE ABSENCE OF MORAL STANDARDS
  (Awarded not for shagging the sheep, but for not respecting her the following morning.)
- ED YOUNG – THE VINCE DOUGLAS FOUL-MOUTHED CUNT CUP
- SUSI JUDGE-DAVIS – THE ENA SHARPLES GOLDEN HAIRNET FOR BEST USE OF HIGH-VOLTAGE CURLING TONGS
- SUSI JUDGE-DAVIS – THE VICTORIA BECKHAM 'YOU MAKE *ME* LOOK FAT, YOU COW' SILVER CELERY STICK
- NIGEL GODLEY – THE PERTTI VAN HELDEN PALM D'OR FOR LIFETIME NON-ACHIEVEMENT

I sincerely believe that all the winners have done Miller Shanks proud.

Finally, massive respect to whoever left the Grade 1 Colombian on my desk. Top gear, dude!

Nige

Harriet Greenbaum – 15/12/00, 11.24am
to... Rachel Stevenson
cc...
re... that e-mail

In addition to finding the perpetrator of the fake awards, get me the bastard who wrote that e-mail – Godley might have the nerve but certainly not the wit. As soon as you find out, bring me his/her head.

brett_topowlski@tbwa.co.uk
15/12/00, 11.33am
to... liam_okeefe@millershanks-london.co.uk
cc...
re... alibi

So, you cheating gobshite, who the fuck was she? As for Vin, I've got a serious case of denial on my hands. Whatever he did, he's blanked it out. The last time this happened was after Berlin, last New Year. When I finally dragged the truth out of him then, it involved a double amputee and golden showers. I dread to fucking think what he's been up to now. By the way, congrats on your new Euro CEO. Only Miller Shanks could give that job to Champion the Wonder Norse ('*Ein reich, ein volk, ein Pertti*'). Crutton looked pretty irate, even by his exceptionally high standards. Anyone would think he wanted the job. Gotta go. Vin's just gone into shock – rocking back and forth in a foetal position on his chair. I'm off to the caff to get him sweet tea.

Wanda Bragg – 15/12/00, 11.40am
to... Liam O'Keefe
cc...
re... fair play 2 u

kool e
it was u wasnt it
?
incidentally
u plan 2 blank me all day
?
w&a

Ken Perry – 15/12/00, 11.42am
to... All Departments
cc...
re... car park

Due to flooding caused by the unscheduled activation of the sprinkler system, the car park will be out of service until further notice.

My apologies for the inconvenience and thank you for your co-operation.

Ken Perry

Office Administrator

Harriet Greenbaum – 15/12/00, 11.47am
to... Zoë Clarke
cc...
re... Katie Philpott

Find her now. I would like her to give me a bloody good explanation as to why her aunt set off the sprinklers on her way out. Tell her I am taking this personally – from what Ken Perry tells me, I could now open an aquarium in my Mercedes.

Nigel Godley – 15/12/00, 12.11pm
to... Rachel Stevenson
cc...
re... I demand justice

I have just returned to my desk and seen that e-mail in my 'sent' file. This is an outrage. I demand that the perpetrator is found and obliged to make an unconditional apology for this slur on my good name. My future presence at Miller Shanks depends upon you pursuing this matter with utmost urgency.

Incidentally, I have typed this with rubber gloves, should the investigating authorities wish to dust my keyboard for finger prints.

Nige

Melinda Sheridan – 15/12/00, 12.13pm
to... Harriet Greenbaum
cc...
re... update

Harriet, sorry to hear about your car – just what you needed this morning. Anyway, I've made a little progress since our chat, so perhaps it will improve your mood.

I have told Ed Young that the band won't be receiving payment for last night. Beyond the torrent of abuse he showered me with, I expect no further comebacks.

And Vinnie Jones is being as sweet as pie over the contretemps with our Director of Resource and Training. He says he was more surprised than anything. ('I was only giving the oily little fucker his prize. I've been whacked by enough hairy-arsed footballers. It makes a nice fucking change to get one off a toffee-nosed twat,' were his exact words.) He puts it down to high spirits that go with the time of year. You might like to mention to Dan that, apparently, he punches like a girl. When you see him, that is. I hear he won't be in until Monday, earliest – broken middle and index fingers.

Once again, I can't apologise enough for my part in last night's 'misadventures'. At least, as you discovered at the Marriott, most of our Continental colleagues were too pissed and/or linguistically challenged to work out what the hell was going on. And, if it's any consolation, the buzz on the shop floor is that it was the best party in donkeys' years.

Liam O'Keefe – 15/12/00, 12.16pm
to... Wanda Bragg
cc...
re... fair play 2 u

Course I'm not blanking you. It's just a bit awkward. It's not
that I didn't enjoy it or anything. But could we, you know, act
like it didn't happen, not mention it again, blah, blah, blah ...
you know the kind of thing. Look, we can still be mates. I
really, really like you and everything.

Zoë Clarke – 15/12/00, 12.18pm
to... Lorraine Pallister; Debbie Wright
cc...
re... no news

Asked the whole bloody agency and no-one has a clue who
Vin was doing!!!! Unbelievable that no-one saw anything
apart from that one little snog with me!!!!!!!!!! And I didn't
shag him!! DIDN'T, DIDN'T, DIDN'T!!!!!!!!!!! You two found
anything out? Won't be able to make lunch. Got to find
mechanics and valets for Harriet's car ... Zx

Rachel Stevenson – 15/12/00, 12.20pm
to... Harriet Greenbaum
cc...
re... that e-mail

Although Nigel has cordoned off his desk like a crime scene
(heaven knows where he got the yellow tape), I don't hold out
much hope of finding the culprit. I think it's fairly certain that
the author of the e-mail and the deviser of the awards are one
and the same. Like you, I have my suspicions but we can't do
anything without clear evidence. For now I suggest you have a

discreet word with Pinki about keeping a close watch on Liam and his friends.

Wanda Bragg – 15/12/00, 12.24pm
to... Liam O'Keefe
cc...
re... fair play 2 u

id say fuck u
but i already did that
still friends
?
of course
u r 2 crap at sex 2 b anything else
w&a

pertti_vanhelden@millershanks-helsinki.co.fi
15/12/00, 4.47pm (6.47pm local)
to... all_departments@millershanks-london.co.uk
cc...
re... thanking you letter

I am just arriving back at my office and still my head is reeling with memory of your warmth and hospitalisation last evening. That, my pals, was some party! And I am speaking as a citizen of a country famous for its 'pissing-ups'!

It is filling me with hopes for the best for when I am joining you in your London premises in the new year as your European Top Cheese. I think that you will 'a-gruyere' that we will 'a-cheese' 'grated' things together!

I am hoping that Santa is emptying his sacks up all your chimney places.

Pertti

Susi Judge-Davis – 15/12/00, 5.00pm
to... Katie Philpott
cc...
re... nightmare

Sorry, Katie, been feeling far too yucky to face office today. Only sneaked in to get things for weekend. Can't remember single thing that happened last night. Never been blotto before. If that's what it's like, never again!!! Got to go. Going to throw up again.

Friday
22 December
2000

Susi Judge-Davis – 22/12/00, 11.27am
to... Katie Philpott
cc...
re... HELP!!!!!!!

YOU'VE GOT TO COME HERE NOW AND TELL ME IF A
BLUE LINE ON ONE OF THOSE STUPID STICKS YOU
WEE ON MEANS WHAT I THINK IT DOES!!!!!!!!!!

e

Matt Beaumont

e is a tapestry of insincerity, backstabbing and bare-faced bitchiness – just everyday office politics.

Meet:

- a CEO with an MBA from the Joseph Stalin School of Management
- a director who is a genius, if only in his own head
- creatives with remarkable brains, if only in their trousers
- a copywriter with the two things no adwoman should ever show – underarm hair and a conscience
- secretaries who drip honey and spit cyanide
- the sad git in accounts

Consisting entirely of e-mails, *e* spends a week in the company of Miller Shanks, an advertising agency embarked upon the quest to land Coca-Cola – the account they would sell their collective grandmothers in a car boot sale to acquire. This is one pitch that nobody will ever forget . . .

'Depicts the Machiavellian scheming and summary sackings of the ad world in withering detail and with no shortage of dead-eye wit'   *The Times*

'Groundbreaking . . . an internet-enabled *Clarissa* for the 21st century'   *Evening Standard*

ISBN 0 00 710068 X

For further adventures in adland,
competitions and extra information, go to:
www.millershanks.com